Slow Train to Nowhere: Sean

by

Laura Strickland

Slow Train to Nowhere, Book 1

Slow Train to Nowhere: Sean

Cover Art by *Tina Lynn Stout*

The Wild Rose Press, Inc.
PO Box 708
Adams Basin, NY 14410-0708
Visit us at www.thewildrosepress.com

Publishing History
First Edition, 2024
Trade Paperback ISBN 978-1-5092-5506-1
Digital ISBN 978-1-5092-5507-8

Slow Train to Nowhere, Book 1
Published in the United States of America

Prologue

Clabber Mills, Indiana, 1860

The five children stood holding hands in a ragged row on the wooden platform of the train station. They differed almost comically in size from the tallest, a boy with sandy hair and freckles who had so outgrown his trousers they looked like pantaloons, to a tiny, dark-haired girl who, had she not been clutching the hands of her two neighbors, might well have been sucking her thumb. They all shared one thing, the shocked, wide-eyed stare of a calf being led to the slaughter.

Behind them the train puffed steam and shuddered in place, for it had not reached its final destination and waited to leave. This small town of Clabber Mills, Indiana was just a brief stop for it to disgorge a number of passengers before abandoning them to their fates.

The sun beat down mercilessly on the five heads—the sandy, the dark, and three of varying shades of brown—from a cloudless sky. At a deliberate distance from the children stood a woman in dark clothing, so tightly-laced she refused to sweat. Beneath a plain, navy-blue bonnet her face had drawn up like a purse, her pale eyes searching the townsfolk coming and going from the station, for anyone bent on meeting her charges.

"Where are we?" asked one of the two brown-haired girls, her voice wavering despite her best efforts.

"What's gonna happen to us?"

"Silence," called Mrs. Kendall, who, though she had distanced herself, was still patently in charge of them. "What did I tell you about speaking out of turn? Nobody likes a chatterbox."

The girl, named Sarah Tate, glanced at the taller boy, who stood next to her in line. He directed a stare back at her from pale gray eyes. A warning. He didn't know precisely what was happening, but he had a pretty fair idea and it wasn't good.

The train had stopped at other towns along the way west and at each one had spit out a handful of other children. Sometimes six or seven, sometimes as few as two. Sean had watched from the window of the train car for as long as it remained at those stations and observed what happened to some of those children.

People came for them. People in buckboards. Or riding horses. Some on foot. They came and took those children away.

He had no doubt whatsoever that would now happen to the five of them. Was that not why the Service, as those in charge called it—more properly the Service for Unwanted Children—had brought them west?

He wasn't stupid no matter what the folks in charge of the Service thought, and he'd kept his ears open ever since getting hauled in off the streets back in New York. The big wigs in charge of the Service hadn't sat anybody down and explained their intentions. Children, so Sean gathered, didn't warrant an explanation of their intended fates. Neither had they made a particular secret of it. They took problem children off the streets of New York and sent them west to families that wanted them.

Sean shifted his feet on the platform, feeling the heat

of the boards right up through his thin-soled shoes. Sweat trickled down his face from beneath his cap and made tracks on his chest and between his shoulder blades. He narrowed his eyes against the glare.

In his opinion, the folks who ran the Service were idiots. Sure, there were a lot of kids running the streets back home. Many, like the four who stood beside him, were orphans.

He was not.

He'd tried to tell the folks at the Service that when they'd picked him up. He'd said he had a pa who would be missing him, looking for him, even though it was partly a lie. Pa, in a tavern somewhere, would likely take some time to figure that Sean was gone.

Still, he was no orphan and he'd tried to make a point of that. He'd been told he was a troublemaker running with a gang of other boys, stealing from market stalls and causing mayhem. That was the word the pitiless woman back in New York had used.

Sean hadn't known what that meant. He ran with other boys in order to survive. He stole because he needed to eat.

He was eleven years old, though he looked older because of his height. He remembered all of his past lives. One in Ireland where they'd been starving. He remembered the voyage across to New York and Ma dying on the way. He remembered the perilous existence in New York, Pa looking for work and unable to find it because he was drunk half the time.

More than half the time.

The way Sean saw it, he'd now been pressed—just like the gangs who came and took sailors away against their will. He'd be imprisoned and made to work here in this new hell.

He was Sean Hussey. He was his own man.

Little Rosalee began to cry. The smallest of them, they'd tucked her into the center of the line, though Sean doubted they'd be able to protect her much longer.

What if they got separated? The kids at the other stops had.

He didn't know his companions all that well. He'd seen them at the Service headquarters and been with them on the train. He'd sat with the other boy, Milo, for a while. Still, once the hideous Mrs. Kendall abandoned them, they would be all each other had here in this foreign place.

Piteously, Rosalee wailed, "I need the outhouse." Rosalee spoke only broken English and had come from somewhere far away. Italy, maybe. Sean pegged her at about six years old.

Mrs. Kendall moved forward. She bent and hollered into Rosalee's face, "You will stand here, child, and be silent. Your new parents are coming for you. If you pee your pants again, I will smack you so hard you'll be sorry."

Sean turned, never leaving go of the hand of Sarah Tate, who stood beside him. "If you hit her," he told Mrs. Kendall in a fierce undertone, "I'll hit ye back still harder."

She abandoned poor Rosalee to straighten and glare into Sean's face. Her eyes looked colder than a northern sea.

"You are an evil boy, Sean Hussey, and I pity the family who takes you on."

Someone cleared his throat behind Mrs. Kendall. A buckboard had rumbled up alongside the platform and a man had alighted.

Sean's first look at Bennie Clabber.

A big rawboned man he was, with broad shoulders, light brown hair, and a heavy, ugly face. Sean would come to hate that face and hate the man's ham fists even more. He did not know that then but sensed it instinctively with the same brand of self-preservation that had kept him alive on the streets for nearly a year.

Mrs. Kendall spun. "Mr. Clabber?" she asked brightly in a far different voice than she used with the children.

Mr. Clabber grunted and eyed Sean up and down. "This him? The one meant for me? Trouble, is he?" He spat into the dirt beside the platform. "We'll soon sort that out."

Mrs. Kendall produced a sheet of paper and consulted it. "This is Sean Hussey, and yes, he's slotted for you."

"Shawn?" Mr. Clabber balked. "What kind o' heathen name is that?"

"I believe it means John," Mrs. Kendall said sweetly.

"Then *John*'s what I'll call him. He'll not go by any ungodly name on good Christian soil." He growled at Sean. "Come with me, boy."

A sickening wave of panic poured through Sean. He'd felt nothing like it since the crossing when Ma had died, when he'd stood beside Pa and watched her shrouded figure go over the side into the depthless waters. *She's gone to join all your brothers and sisters*, Pa had said, for Sean was her last surviving child.

Ma, who had called him Sean.

Sean he was.

"Come along, I said." Clabber reached out and almost casually whacked Sean on the side of the head. Sean didn't fall down, but he saw stars.

His four companions immediately started to protest. He'd been their protector. Now they sought to defend him.

Sarah, at his side, did not want to let go of his hand. She clung to his fingers even as Clabber pulled him away.

Sean turned and looked into her eyes. Blue eyes they were, now awash with tears.

"Be brave," he told her. "All o' ye, be brave."

Chapter One

Clabber Mills, Indiana, 1875

The man stood on the wooden platform beside the Clabber Mills train station, bathed in strong sunlight. Tall and lean with sandy-brown hair and a tanned complexion, he wore a brown hat that looked new and a pair of boots that didn't. Several other passengers had disembarked from the train along with him. Most had swiftly gathered their bags and hurried off. He alone stood where he'd landed, a certain stillness about him.

It looked just the same, did the small town of Clabber Mills. The same as it had fifteen years ago when he'd set foot here for the first time. Too much the same. He'd hoped—in the limited way he still possessed a capacity for hoping—he wouldn't recognize the place. That some catastrophic change might have taken place that would render what he'd come back to do unnecessary.

No such luck.

Folks hurried by, and the station master strolled past, giving him a sharp look. The man as swiftly looked away again, finding something in the eyes of the new arrival as well as his preternatural stillness off-putting.

Would anybody recognize him? He doubted it. Fifteen years, yes, had passed since he'd stepped onto this platform for the first time, and ten since he'd left here, with five years of hell between.

The sun beat down on his head like a hammer. He remembered that about this town. The weather was as merciless as everything else about the place. When it rained, it could half drown a man or a boy. When it was hot, it could fair scorch him. In winter when the cold came, it could freeze off pieces of his fingers.

Of all the places he'd seen during his travels over the years following his escape, he hated this seemingly innocuous town the most.

Quite fitting, then, that he'd returned only to kill a man and leave again.

He nudged the single bag that lay at his feet with his toe, and a figure across the way caught his eye. A young man of medium height with broad shoulders and a crop of rich brown hair that shone in the sun. The fellow had just drawn up a wagon opposite the station and leaped down in a fluid movement to approach the platform. His gaze fixed on the new arrival and did not waver.

"John?" he asked, leaping up onto the platform and facing the taller man.

"It's Sean, Digger."

A grin split the young man's face, one that Sean recognized. Suddenly he was back in that other life long ago with the lad Milo Digsby, who'd ridden the train to nowhere in his company.

The grin was the same, wide and winsome. The crinkle of the brown eyes, on the face of the man, might have been that of the boy he'd been.

"How the hell are you?" To Sean's surprise, Digger threw an arm around him and thumped him on the back heartily. "God damn it, man, till I got your letter I thought you must be dead."

Sean nodded. He'd written the letter last winter after he'd made up his mind what he had to do. He'd decided trying to contact Milo—Digger—would be the best bet. The girls could all be married by now and would have changed their names.

It had taken Milo a while to answer, and they'd written back and forth a few times, neither of them a dab hand with a pen. Their letters had been brief and to the point, and had contained few details.

Milo eyed Sean, clearly taking his measure. "Not sure I would have recognized you."

"Nor me, you. You've grown. A lot."

Milo made a face. "I was a puny kid. Caught up in my teens."

Sean nodded soberly. Very few good memories dwelt in his head. "So, Digger, how have you been?"

"Nobody calls me Digger anymore. Not since you left." A bleak expression invaded Milo's fine brown eyes.

They'd called him Digger because of his last name—Digsby—and because he'd had a tendency when distressed to dig holes in the brown dirt of this place and try to crawl into them.

They'd all wanted to disappear back then.

"I'm doin' all right. What about you? Where've you been?"

"Everywhere. Out west mostly." Sean did not want to talk about that. "How are the girls?"

Caution flooded Milo's eyes. "Rosalee's engaged to be married."

"Just like you." Milo had written that much in his letter. He was set to marry Temperance Bligh, the daughter of the man he'd gone to work for when they'd landed here so long ago.

Both he and Milo had gone to work for farmers, as did most lads who came out on the orphan trains.

"Sarah—well, Sarah's a widow."

"Young to be widowed, ain't she?"

"Yeah. Husband was trampled by a runaway team. She's got a young boy." A new look invaded Milo's eyes. "She's had trouble taking care of herself and him."

Maybe he could help. That thought came unbidden to Sean's mind. He wasn't sure why, because in the past he'd never been able to do anything to help any of them. But he had money now, a good portion of it nestled in the bag at his feet.

And Jenny? He didn't want to ask. He desperately wanted to know.

As if he'd heard the thought, Milo said, "Of course Jenny's married."

"Is she?" Sean's whole body stiffened.

Milo's eyes now turned troubled. "To a right bastard."

Sean went cold all over, an occurrence he recognized. Maybe he could do something to help after all. He'd returned to Clabber Mills in order to kill a man. Nothing to say he couldn't kill two.

****

"Come on." Milo thumped him on the back again. "I'll buy you a drink. You can tell me all about your life."

It felt good to get in out of the blinding sunlight, even though the interior of the saloon smelled like spilled beer and unwashed farmhand. Over the years, Sean had frequented more places of this ilk than he could easily count. Raucous saloons out west and some along the train lines that set themselves up as more sophisticated.

In the days past, when he'd lived in Clabber Mills, Sean had never set foot in here. Bennie Clabber would have beaten him bloody.

He'd beaten him bloody anyway.

At this hour, the saloon contained only a few customers. He and Milo sat at a table on one side where Milo eyed Sean with caution and said, "You're wearin' a gun."

He must have caught sight of the weapon when Sean sat down.

"Yeah."

"You took that up, did you, after you lit out?"

"I did."

The bartender brought over two beers with a curious look at Sean. Milo didn't speak till the fellow retreated out of earshot.

"I confess, I thought when you ran away you'd go back to New York. It was what we all wanted in them days, wasn't it? To go home."

"I thought about it." Sean took a slug of his beer. It was second rate. Second rate beer in a third-rate town.

"I've gotta say, I can't count the nights I longed for home after I went to live with the Blighs. Would have cut off my own right arm to get out of this place."

"I know." They'd all felt like that. Little Rosalee had sobbed till she made herself sick and a doctor had to be called, even though the Thompsons, who'd taken her in, had treated her like a favored pet.

Sean had been required to toughen up a lot faster than that.

He told Milo, "I decided there wasn't really anything to go back to in New York. It wasn't home, was it?" He'd never had a home save back in Ireland when

Ma was alive.

"You had your pa." Milo gulped beer. "More than I had." Something hot kindled in Milo's expressive eyes. "It still makes me mad, the way the Society snatched us and sent us away as if they owned us. Even though some of us, like you, still had parents."

Sean shrugged, pretending it didn't bother him. A long time ago. And if his pa had wanted him, he'd have stopped drinking.

"You know, they told our neighbor—the one who tried to look after me after my pa got sick and died—they were snatching me. She tried to speak up for me, even said she'd look out for me. But she was working in a sweatshop and her own kids were barely surviving. Those folks from the Society convinced her she'd be giving me a better chance if I came west."

"You were runnin' the streets just like I was." Though they hadn't known each other then. "The big wigs in New York, they didn't like Irish brats—or any other kind—making their streets untidy." Sean hesitated two beats. "You ever think of goin' back to look for anybody you knew, back there?"

"I've given it a lot of thought, if I'm honest." Milo frowned, somehow looking like the lad Digger once again. "Wouldn't begin to know how to find anybody."

"No." Sean drank more beer. It tasted worse this time.

"Besides," Milo said uneasily, "there were always the Blighs."

Sean raised his eyes and searched the face of his companion. The Blighs had collected Milo that first day when they'd all stood on the platform. A fiercely straight-laced, God-fearing family with three daughters and another boy they'd had off a previous orphan train, they'd taken the raising of children very seriously and church going more seriously still.

The way Sean remembered it, and he'd had nearly five years to observe before leaving Clabber Mills, the Blighs had treated both Milo and their other ward, Chuck, neither like members of the family nor like servants. Something in between. He had, of course, mainly seen Milo at school when their farm chores permitted them to attend. And at the few church functions to which Bennie Clabber had taken Sean. Or John, as he'd insisted on calling him.

He set his mug back down on the table. "Can I ask how you came to be engaged to the Blighs' daughter?"

Milo looked uneasy. "You remember, the Blighs had no sons."

"Of their own."

"Of their own. Old Emmanuel Bligh prayed on it and eventually decided Chuck should marry Patience, the oldest daughter, to keep the farm in the family. Chuck had other ideas. He ran off before being dragged to the altar."

"I don't blame him." Sean remembered Patience from school. A horrible, prissy girl with a cast in one eye. Of course, a person couldn't help their physical disadvantages. But she sure might have improved her personality.

"Patience eventually married someone else and moved away. Mr. Bligh tried to convince me to look at Charity, but she took up with a soldier out of Fort Davis and wouldn't rest till she'd married him. That left Temperance. And me." Milo made a face. "Soon's she grew old enough, old Bligh told me he was doing me a great honor. I could marry her and inherit the farm once he'd gone to his glorious reward."

Sean couldn't help but stare. "He wanted to make you a member of the family?"

Milo shrugged. "More or less."

"And this is what you want?"

For the first time Milo's eyes became guarded. "Temperance isn't so bad. And it's a good place, John—Sean. Better than anything I ever dreamed I'd own."

Would he own it, though? Or would he be, in old Bligh's eyes, a stand-in for the children Temperance would one day birth?

None of his, Sean's, business if Milo wanted to toss away what remained of his life.

"As I live and breathe, it's Sean Hussey!" A voice sounded beside him.

He looked up from the table and met Sarah Tate's eyes.

Chapter Two

Sarah noticed the men as soon as she came down from the rooms upstairs, two of them sitting together at the table in the corner. Milo Digsby she knew—she considered him among her few friends, which at this point she could count on one hand.

Something about the other man, who sat facing Milo, forced all the breath from her lungs. *It couldn't be. By God, it could not be.*

How unlikely that he would return after an absence of ten years. And he looked so different—a man full grown sitting in his seat so tall. The last time she'd seen Sean Hussey he'd been a scrawny boy, tall for his age but with hunger in the set of his limbs and in his eyes.

A terrible hunger.

Curiosity and a queer kind of longing drew her to their table. She eyed his profile which, yes, had something familiar about it. The stubborn set to the slightly square chin. The stark slant of the one cheekbone she could see. The straight, almost pugnacious nose.

Could this be Sean Hussey all grown? If he looked at her—if she saw those pale gray eyes—she'd know for sure.

But did she truly want him to look at her and see how far she'd fallen?

She spoke in an effort of defiance against that thought. "As I live and breathe, it's Sean Hussey."

He looked up at her, the tan hat he wore tilting so she got a good gander at him. For the space of five or six heartbeats they regarded one another.

Then Milo said, "Sarah. Sean, it's Sarah."

Did Sean look shocked? The gray gaze, which looked colder than she remembered, performed a swift inspection of her, no doubt taking in the details. A brief appraisal but an accurate one. Sean Hussey had never been stupid.

Just one of the things she'd admired about him.

"Sarah," he said and half got to his feet, a mark of respect.

"What in tarnation are you doing back in Clabber Mills?" She wetted her lips. "Didn't suppose we'd ever see you again." *Though she'd hoped.*

"Only a fool would come back, right?"

"For sure."

He hadn't answered the question, but Sarah was far too overwhelmed at seeing him to push for it.

He'd grown. Finished growing into a tall, attractive man. Not handsome by any means, but there was strength in those broad, heavy cheekbones and the set of his jaw. And she'd had her fill of weak men. Oh, by God, she had.

Maybe—just maybe—he'd grown into the man she'd always known he could be.

"You plan on staying long in Clabber Mills?"

"Don't rightly know as yet." He'd lost nearly all the Irish that had colored his voice when they'd met back on the orphan train, though it still lurked a bit in the vowels and the ends of the words.

"You back for business?"

Something glinted in those pale eyes. "That's right.

To take care o' business."

"Mind if I sit down?" Sarah glanced at the bar. "Stu, I'll have a rye. Take it off my allowance."

Sean didn't change expression, though yes, he had to be shocked by that and by the dress she had on—a frilly piece fit for a trollop. Which was what she'd become.

She sat down and the bartender brought the drink which she didn't touch.

"You work here?" Sean asked.

"Work. And live." She jerked her head. "Upstairs."

"Digger tells me you're a widow."

Digger. She hadn't heard that in years. He really was Sean.

"Yeah" She tried to make it sound careless. "Married a man called Ben Rupert. A team of runaway horses did me a terrible disservice and ran him down. Though in truth he wasn't that much of a husband."

"I liked Ben," Milo said suddenly. "He had his good side."

"He did." Sarah blinked as she fought back the tangled emotions roused by the mention of her husband. "Left me with nothing except a son to raise." She lifted her eyes to Sean defiantly. "That's why I'm here."

Milo spoke again. Milo, always the peacemaker who just wanted to get along. Not a weakness in his case, but a strength forged by necessity. "Couldn't the Gregsons help you, Sarah? You lived with them all that time. And, well, it would have to be better than—this."

"No," Sarah told him readily. If she never saw Thaddeus Gregson again it would be too soon. But she could never confide in Milo, with his earnest gaze. Milo, who'd sold his soul to belong.

"How old's your boy?" Sean asked.

"Nearly eight. Name's Luke."

"He lives with you here?"

"I have a friend who boards him for me. She has a little boy too. He's there now." Her face tightened. "My shift starts soon."

"I'm sorry, Sarah." Sean seemed to struggle for words. "Sorry for your losses."

She tossed her head. "Life was never good since we got here, was it? Not for any of us. Least of all you. Well, maybe Rosalee didn't fare too badly. The Thompsons were right good to her. She was always such a pretty little thing."

"Still is," Milo put in and Sarah glanced at him sharply. She'd often wondered a little about Milo and Rosalee.

Of course any man engaged in marriage to a female like Temperance Bligh couldn't be blamed for turning his eyes anywhere else.

"So," she asked Sean, "what you been up to all these years?"

"Went out west. Started a business with a partner."

"What sort of business?" Sarah raised her eyebrows. His clothing was good, expensive. Only his boots looked worn. And was that a gun he wore at his hip?

"Shipping merchandise. Moving it from back east."

"Well, aren't you the success story? You ever go home?"

That made him fix his eyes to hers. "To New York? Or Ireland?"

Milo stepped in. "We was just talking about that. New York, I mean. Not much to go back for."

"True. You never thought of going back to Ireland

either?" she asked Sean.

"Probably not much left there either. Don't know my people after all these years."

Sarah leaned her chin on her hand. When she sat so of an evening, men usually took advantage in order to eye her bosom. Sean didn't even glance in that direction.

"We truly were cut adrift, weren't we?" she mused. "Loaded on that train and scattered out like seeds."

"Some good seeds, some bad." Sean agreed.

She wondered to which of them he referred. Her? Himself?

"Are you thinking of moving your business here to Clabber Mills?"

"No. God, no. Just—I felt the itch to tie up some loose ends."

That made her narrow her eyes at him. She wondered if he meant Bennie Clabber. The bastard had been vile toward Sean. She'd seen the bruises and scrapes at school. Well, they'd all had bruises.

Maybe Sean had come to gloat over Bennie, flaunt his success a little.

"Where you planning to stay?"

"I invited him to bunk with me at the farm. The Blighs wouldn't mind."

Sarah looked at Milo with sympathy. "Out in the barn, you mean?" Where the Blighs let him sleep. Where they'd always let him sleep.

"Sure. It's comfortable enough."

"Just think." Sarah got to her feet. She still hadn't touched her drink. "Once you and Temperance get married, you'll be able to move into the house." She tweaked his nose. "Like a good boy."

Milo gazed at her with mute misery.

19

"Sarah," Sean said, "why ride him? He's made his choice."

"We've all made a lot of choices. The trick is living with them afterward. You lot—" to her horror, tears came to her eyes, "why, apart from Luke you're the closest thing I have to family. I just don't like seeing Milo make a mistake."

"It's not a mistake," Milo said gently.

"Of course not." Sarah switched her gaze back to Sean and tried to summon up a smile. "If you want to stop back later, anytime while you're in town—" She left it hanging suggestively.

"I might do that." Then he did something that shocked her to the core. Caught one of her hands in his and raised it to his lips. Planted a kiss on the knuckles. "Sarah."

Never, never had she been treated so. Not even by Ben. She snatched her hand away and hid it in the skirt of her tawdry dress. Gave Milo a startled look before she moved off, leaving her drink behind.

Chapter Three

"So what's Sarah's story?" Sean asked Milo as soon as she had walked away. "How'd she end up here?"

"She just explained it, didn't she?" Milo's eyes went blank. "Husband dead. Left her with nothing."

"There had to be something better than this." Sean had liked Sarah from the first she'd been brought from the girls' quarters at the Society and loaded onto the train. She couldn't have been more than ten and had been tall for her age, like him. Plain, light brown hair and clear blue eyes. A tendency to keep quiet and not make a fuss.

Some things had changed.

Despite her clothing, he would have recognized her anywhere, though God knew she was no longer the pale, silent girl with whom he'd shared the station platform that day.

Milo shrugged. "Not much here for a widow."

Anything would be better than whoring. He'd been grateful for the attentions of whores more than a few times. He'd struggled, though, to keep himself from seeing his encounters with them through their eyes. "Can't she sew? Get a job cooking some place?"

"Don't know. The Gregsons cast her off after she married Ben. That was some nine years ago."

"That long?" Sarah must have married shortly after Sean left town. Funny, he didn't remember this Ben Rupert. "She couldn't have been very old."

21

"About sixteen? Seventeen maybe? I think she wanted to get away from the Gregsons."

Hadn't they all wanted to escape the families that had taken them in? With the exception of Rosalee, and Milo who apparently thought it a good thing to marry into the family that for years had treated him like a dog.

With some difficulty, he moved his thoughts away from Sarah. "So when's your wedding?"

"Later this fall. After the harvest's all in." Milo's face suddenly lit. "Maybe you can attend. I sure would like for you to be there. Maybe you could stand up with me."

Sean drank the last of his lukewarm beer. "Don't know if I'll be in town that long." As Milo's face fell, he added, "If I am, I sure will stand up with you, Milo. I'd be proud."

"The marriage—it's a good choice on my part, Sean. I know it might not seem like it."

"They never treated you well, Digger."

"Don't you see? In a way this makes up for it. The farm's grown since you left, Sean. It's more than I ever dreamed I could own. I've put a lot of my sweat into that place. This is a chance to get something back for that."

Sean studied his friend carefully. In the old days he would have said Milo Digsby was one of the last people to make a choice for the sake of wealth. To old Bligh, he would be little more than a stud horse standing in for his daughter, Temperance. It saddened him to see Digger dedicate his life to gain rather than—well, love.

But then they hadn't seen much of love, had they?

As if he heard Sean's thoughts, Milo leaned across the table and lowered his voice. "Once old Bligh is dead, Sean, it will all be mine. He can't live forever."

"No." It might just seem like it.

****

He told Milo as kindly as possible that he couldn't stay with him in his room at the barn. He appreciated the invitation more than he could say, but if he got out there, if he saw the Blighs treating Digger the way they used to, he might lose his temper and do something foolish.

Instead, since Milo seemed eager to show him the place, he promised to come out and visit.

As soon as Milo left with the Blighs' wagon and team, Sean walked out into the sunlight. It had grown hotter than ever, but he walked around town anyway, taking stock of the changes.

Clabber Mills had never been a large town, just a stop on the rails that trailed ever westward seemingly to nowhere.

In the town's early days there hadn't been much more than the mill, bult by a man called Clabber, at the place where the river took a short fall. He hadn't been the same Clabber who'd taken Sean in, but his uncle. A number of Clabbers had followed the first to settle. Bennie Clabber's father had been a farmer.

From what he could see, the mill looked busy and must still be thriving. In addition the town sported the school where he and the others had suffered and the church where he'd sat through only an occasional sermon. What had used to be a trading post had grown into a general store. A feed store stood beside it and not much else. The Three Feathers saloon where he'd met Sarah seemed to be the only one in town.

Clabber Mills was a God-fearing sort of community. He doubted they'd tolerate more than one saloon.

But having turned down Milo's kind offer of

hospitality, he didn't know where he was going to stay.

He wandered into the general store thinking to ask about rooms. Again, the large wooden building gave some relief from the fierce sun. He stood for a minute while his eyes adjusted to the dim light.

At this time of day, early afternoon, the store was busy. Several ladies inspected yard goods and a man in a shopkeeper's apron showed a fellow some tools. Behind the counter stood a sour-faced woman whom Sean approached with a smile.

Sometimes his smiles worked, and sometimes they didn't. He'd been told by a woman he met once in a saloon out west that his smile never reached his eyes. *You've got the coldest eyes I've ever seen.*

In this case, the sour-faced woman, a lady of middle years, stared at him as if instead of smiling he'd suggested something obscene.

"Ma'am, I'm wondering if you can help me."

She eyed him up and down. No doubt noted the quality of his coat, of his hat, which he'd bought new for this very trip.

Did he know her? Ten years ago when he'd left Clabber Mills, the Bensons had run the store. He did not see either of them now.

"Yes?" she said, barely polite.

"I just arrived in town and I'm looking for a place to stay."

"This is a store, mister, not a rooming house."

"I can see that. But I thought you might know of a place with rooms to let. I even thought," he leaned toward her a bit, "you might have a notice up or some such."

"Well, I don't."

"You don't have a notice up, or you don't know of any place?"

She sniffed. "Either." She inspected him again, her eyes prodding at the gun on his hip. "Not for your sort."

"Cora? What's the problem?" The shopkeeper came up, frowning.

"This person wants to rent a room."

"Just for a few days," Sean said evenly. "I was asking the lady if she knew any place." He should have asked at the train station before he left the platform.

The shopkeeper did his own assessment. "No rooming houses here in town. But there are a few householders who let out rooms. Cora, what about Mrs. Dennison?"

"She's got no more'n the one room and that's taken."

"Ah. What about the Withers? Didn't Cyrus say he was wanting to let out their spare room?"

"Don't know if that's taken or not." Cora spoke repressively.

"You go on there, mister," the shopkeeper said. "Cyrus will be working right now, but his wife will likely be able to help you. Just keep walkin' east straight out of town. It's the last house on the right. Painted white."

"Thank you kindly. I'll ask there."

It didn't take him long to reach the edge of town. First the businesses and then the houses dwindled. A man might well miss Clabber Mills if he blinked while riding the train.

The last house on the right was small with a handkerchief garden, very neat. A woman worked at the flower bed out front, hunkered down with her back to Sean in the blazing sun.

As he turned up the walk, he noted the back of her dress had soaked through with sweat. She wore her hair in a bun and looked as neat as her yard.

"Mrs. Withers?"

She got to her feet and turned around. Sean froze in surprise, his heart leaping in his chest.

"Jenny?" Yes he'd know her anywhere, the girl who had occupied his thoughts and some of his dreams for the past ten years. Softly he said, "Jenny Spinner, it's me, Sean."

Chapter Four

"It's Withers now," Jenny said with a hint of what might be defiance or shame. She stood there facing Sean in the bright sunshine and he examined her swiftly, grief blooming in his heart.

She'd grown into a fine-looking woman as he'd always known she would. She'd been a fine-looking lass when he'd left. Built on a smaller scale than Sarah, she nevertheless curved in all the right places. Her brown hair, always full of curl but now confined in that bun, had deepened to a rich auburn in the sun. Her eyes showed the same flash of amber in the brown. Except—

One eye sat surrounded by barely faded bruising, the clear impact of a fist. A hard one.

The grief inside Sean expanded and damn near swallowed him.

"Sean?" she repeated his name as if she could not believe he stood in front of her. "Well, by heaven! I didn't think to see you again."

"Jenny—"

One of her hands, the fingers stained with earth, flew to her cheek as if she would cover the abrasion there. Her wide eyes begged him not to mention it. "Goodness! When did you get back?"

"Just today."

"You here for a visit? Don't say you've come back to stay, not once you got clean away from here."

"Not to stay, no. I've got some business here in town."

Milo had said Jenny was married to a right bastard. Still, Sean hadn't expected this.

"How you been?" he asked gently.

Her hands fluttered wildly and for an instant he saw a reflection of what he'd glimpsed in Sarah's eyes. He recognized that emotion because he'd felt it so often. Despair mixed with a stubborn pride that did not want to admit just how terrible things were.

"I—" She ran out of words or perhaps out of lies. For an instant she looked so much like the young girl he'd left standing on the platform when Bennie Clabber dragged him away, he had to swallow hard.

"I—got married."

"So Milo said."

"But what about you? After you ran away, you can't imagine how we wondered. If you were alive or dead. If you'd made it good somehow."

"I did." He set his bag down at his feet. "I did make it good."

"Well, that's wonderful!"

"Your husband ain't home?"

"No. No, he's working. At the mill. It's a good job."

Sean eyed her up and down. "Any kids?"

"No." The color came and went in her face. "Not yet. Cyrus has been hopin'." She drew a breath. "We ain't been married all that long."

"I see."

Jenny looked like she hoped he didn't.

"Man at the general store said you have a room to rent. I need a place to stay while I'm here."

"Oh. Yes."

"Your room still available?"

"It is."

Would it be a good idea for him to stay here, feeling the way he did about her?

"The room ain't much, Sean. Small. And it's hot as Croesus upstairs. Maybe—maybe you'd be better off somewhere else."

"You know of anywhere else?"

She shook her head. A tendril of damp hair escaped the tight bun and curled next to her ear. Pretty little Jenny.

"Maybe you can let me see the room."

She twisted her hands together in front of her. "Cyrus would be real happy to get it rented out."

And Sean just bet she lived to keep Cyrus happy.

****

The interior of the little house was as neat as the front garden. A small, square parlor with every stick of furniture at rigid attention. An even smaller dining room with a table gleaming from polish. Sean glimpsed a kitchen beyond with the sun shining in. A flight of stairs, bare wood, led upward. Jenny directed Sean there.

"We have just the two rooms," she said as they climbed. "Cyrus says we might as well make some money from the spare one till the kids come along."

Already Sean didn't like Cyrus, and he hadn't even met him.

The heat up at the top of the house was stifling. Nothing but a tiny bare wood hallway and two doors opening off it. Jenny indicated the one on the right and Sean stuck his head inside.

A heat box even though Jenny had the single window wide open, it contained only a bed with a quilted cover and a single chest of drawers. Plain white curtains hung at the window.

"It ain't much," Jenny said again.

It wasn't, and Sean couldn't imagine staying here. He turned back and eyed the woman who stood behind him. That bruise on her face. The vulnerable curve of her lips.

"I'll take it," he said.

"You sure? I think Cyrus wants a dollar a week. That's a lot, and it's why nobody else has rented the room. Of course that includes three meals a day."

"Cooked by you?"

"Yes. Mrs. Riles taught me to cook."

Jenny had gone to a farming couple when they'd got off the train. It hadn't worked out and the woman had passed Jenny to her sister who ran a diner and always needed help. Mrs. Riles had treated Jenny like a slave, running her ragged.

"The diner still open?"

Jenny nodded.

"I can always eat there." Sean's gaze softened. "I wouldn't want to give you any more work than you already have." Her hands, which she still twisted together, looked red and work-worn.

"It's included in the price."

"I'll let you know if I'm gonna eat in or out." He swung his bag into the room and set it on the bare floor.

As he moved, Jenny's eyes fixed on his weapon. "You wear a gun."

"I've been out west. Lots of men there do."

Her eyes flew to his face. "You know how to use it?"

"Yeah, Jenny, I do." He reached into his pocket for his bill fold. "Let me pay you for the room in advance. A dollar, you said?"

Her eyes widened at the number of bills in his wallet. "Yes. But maybe you'd better wait and pay Cyrus."

"Won't he trust you to hold it for him?"

A look of doubt flickered in her eyes but she tucked the bill away in the pocket of her apron. "Come downstairs. I'll make you some tea. We—we can maybe catch up a little before Cyrus comes home."

He followed her back down and into the sunny kitchen, his thoughts racing. He did not want to ask. He didn't know what she'd be willing to admit.

The kitchen, a little less stark and slightly more cheerful than the rest of the house, proved no less immaculate. Bright yellow curtains hung at the window which looked out back, and the table had a checked yellow cloth. The cookstove gleamed as if it had just been blacked.

"Sit on down, Sean," Jenny said. "I'll put the kettle on."

She bustled around, more comfortable here in her own domain. She filled the kettle from the pump at the sink and put it on the stove before filling a plate with shortbread which she set on the table. Not until the tea was made did she come and sit opposite him, summoning a smile.

Here in the bright light, Sean could see all too clearly the bruises that marked her face. Purple just beginning to fade to green. The very sight on her pale skin made his hands curl into fists. He had to consciously relax them in order to pick up his teacup.

"So you've seen Milo?" she asked almost eagerly.

"And Sarah."

"Oh." Her expression changed. "Poor Sarah. I

thought she might take my place at the diner when I got married. It's not the easiest work but would be better than—than what she's doing now. You know what she's doing?"

"I've got a pretty good idea."

"I can't imagine. I just can't. She did try at the diner a short while. It didn't work out with Mrs. Riles. And the Gregsons, you know, they wouldn't take her back—"

"Jenny?"

"What?"

Sean reached across the table and touched her cheek gently. "Jenny, did he do this to you? Your husband?"

She stared at him. "Don't be nice to me, Sean. I—I couldn't bear it." Tears pooled in her beautiful eyes. "It doesn't happen often. And anyway, I deserve it. I'm stupid and slow, and I seldom do anything right—"

"Honey." Appalled, Sean struggled to say anything more. "Honey, that ain't true. It can't be."

"I assure you, it is."

It was a truth that had been taught to all of them who had stood on the train platform that day, except maybe little Rosalee. Pounded into some of them. Not good enough. Not worthy. It had taken him a lot of years away to overcome it.

Now he just had to convince Jenny.

Chapter Five

Sean couldn't wait for Cyrus Withers to get home from his fine job at the mill. He wanted to meet this man who Jenny had described raggedly while sitting there at her kitchen table.

"He's a good man, Sean, in a lot of ways. Steady. A hard worker. Wants to save for us to have a better future. A bigger house one day. When the family comes along—"

She'd stared into the air at nothing, after she said that.

"You say he don't hit you often?"

"Oh, no. Just when I push him, like."

"Push him."

"When I question his decisions. Or when I get something wrong once too often, he can't help but be aggravated. He's very particular about things, is Cyrus. Very—very critical, I guess you might say."

Sean wasn't certain what he expected to see when the paragon did at last arrive home from his day's labor. A hulking, broad-fisted brute maybe. Only Cyrus Withers wasn't that. The man who came swinging along the road and up the walk proved to be of a sneering, whipcord type, shorter than Sean with pale brown hair, mud-colored eyes, and a put-upon expression.

Of course Jenny wasn't more than a slip of a thing herself. Sean wondered if it made Withers feel like a big man when he knocked her around.

Not that he did it often. Just when she deserved it. Christ!

Cyrus came striding into the little white house, and his eyes lit on Sean, the stranger there.

"Cyrus," Jenny said quickly, "this is Mr. Hussey. He's rented the room upstairs."

Cyrus's gaze quickened. It ran over Sean like lightning and noted the gun at his hip before flicking to Jenny. "You get the money?"

She slipped it from the pocket of her apron and handed it to him.

"One week in advance," Sean said, his eyes narrowed on Cyrus's face. "I hope that's all right."

Cyrus darted another look at Jenny. "You should have asked me first. My house, ain't it?"

Sure, Jenny just kept it for him. Like a servant.

"Well I thought—"

Sean interrupted her in a soft voice. "If it's gonna be trouble, you can give me back my money and I'll leave. No hard feelings."

Cyrus's fingers closed convulsively on the dollar. "You can stay the week. We got rules in this house, you understand. It's a decent home, right? You don't bring anybody back here, up in your room. You don't come in early or late."

"What's late?"

"After nine."

"That might be a bit difficult. I have business here in town. Maybe you should give me back my money."

No way was Cyrus parting with that dollar. "Ten, then. I don't want my wife chasing around after guests at all hours."

Guests.

"And you keep respectable. Quiet."

Sean wondered if he was allowed to breathe. If Jenny was, without Cyrus's permission. But he nodded.

"We'll see how the week goes. It goes all right, how long are you planning to stay?"

"Don't know yet."

"Well, somebody else comes along wants a long-term let, I might have to toss you out."

Sean would like to see him try.

Cyrus barked at Jenny, "Supper ready yet?"

"Yes, Cyrus."

"Then let's eat."

Jenny was on her feet through most of that meal, running between the kitchen and the dining room, bringing items Cyrus claimed she'd forgotten. No sooner had she sat and eaten a few bites than Cyrus was finished and she leaped up to clear his plate.

It fair turned Sean's stomach.

He'd seen his share of cruelty during his life. In fact from the time he first set foot in Clabber Mills, it had been his lot. He'd seen little to rival the pettiness of this.

Cyrus thought he had Jenny under his thumb, did he? They'd see about that before Sean left town.

Conversation at the table was near nonexistent. Not till Jenny busied herself clearing the meal away and the two men stepped outside did Sean speak.

"So you work at the mill, do you?"

"Yeah. I'm a personal friend of Mr. Conrad Clabber. His apprentice, you might say."

"Mill still going strong?"

Cyrus shot him a close look. "What d'you know about it?"

Sean figured he might as well come clean. Wouldn't take long for it to get out. "Used to live here in Clabber Mills. Came out on the orphan train."

"Jesus! Another one, like Jenny?" Cyrus's eyes abruptly narrowed. "Did you know my wife back then?"

My wife. Intent lay in the two words, an intent to defend.

"Came out on the same train."

"Jesus," Cyrus said again. "She didn't tell me she knew you."

"Does it matter?"

"I don't know."

"Was a long time ago." No need to tell the man he'd held Jenny in his heart near as long.

"Not sure I want a man here alone with my wife."

Sean gave a careless shrug. "I won't be here much during the day. In fact I'm fixing to go back to town now."

Cyrus eyed him again. "Just so long's you don't make a disturbance when you get back. I'm a hard-working man and need my rest. This don't work out, I will ask you to leave."

"Fine. Just so long as you return the unused portion of my money."

Cyrus scowled. He made Sean jump by suddenly raising his voice. "Woman? Get out here!"

Jenny hurried out, drying her hands on her apron. "Yes, Cyrus?"

Cyrus pointed dramatically to the flower bed that edged the tiny porch where they stood. "I see weeds. Wasn't you supposed to clear them out from these beds?"

"That was my fault," Sean said quickly. "I interrupted your wife when I came asking for a room."

Cyrus gave Sean a look that said he'd like to tear him apart. "You shoulda got back to it," he told Jenny coldly. "Jesus Christ! We got an image to keep up, don't we?"

"I'm sorry, Cyrus. I'll finish there tomorrow."

"See you do."

Jenny slipped back inside without a sound. Sean stood next to Cyrus with his blood boiling. What Milo had said about Jenny's husband definitely wasn't an exaggeration.

"Damn woman," Cyrus muttered. "You give a woman a fine home, she should sure as hell look after it."

Give a man a fine wife, he should look after her also, Sean thought. Cyrus Withers needed a lesson. For Jenny's sake, Sean didn't suppose he could give it to him just yet.

Chapter Six

Sarah had been watching the door of the Three
Feathers ever since it started to get busy wondering—
hoping—Sean would come in. He'd indicated earlier that
he would, but Sarah had learned not to count on things
much in life.

She'd gone to her friend Rachel's house to have
some supper and see her son, Luke, half afraid Sean
would come in while she was gone. She and Rachel had
become friends when they were still girls. As Sarah had
told Sean, Rachel had a son, Danny, near Luke's age, and
the two boys often played together. Rachel's husband,
like most men in town, worked at the mill. He didn't
approve of how Sarah made her living but he liked Luke
and, Sarah hoped, was a good influence on him. Sarah
had no doubt it was mainly for Luke's sake Dan had not
objected to Sarah continuing to visit, and he'd not
forbidden Rachel from watching the boy when Sarah
couldn't. Or from keeping Sarah as a friend.

As if Rachel would listen.

The saloon got busy after work at the mill and the
outlying ranches let out. Man after man came in, but
none of them was Sean Hussey. Sarah circulated and sold
drinks, which was on the face of it her actual job. Mr.
Bracer, who owned The Three Feathers, wanted her to
look pretty and keep the customers buying. If she took
men upstairs, which in truth happened but seldom, he

expected his cut.

Sarah needed all the money she could get because she wanted to move herself out from the room upstairs, which always smelled of stale beer and sometimes of the men who spent time there, and find somewhere she and Luke could be together. Clabber Mills pretended to be a decent sort of town. Whatever she did, she must be discreet. People didn't want her extra duties waved in their faces. Sarah might argue with the *decent* part. Yes, most folks went to the white church down the street. As she'd learned at the age of ten, that didn't always mean much.

When Sean came in, all her senses leapt to attention. She was talking to a table full of what she took as traveling salesmen at the time, one of whom flirted with her outrageously. Mr. Bracer told her to be welcoming, friendly. To look pretty. That last, so she felt, was beyond her. But men seemed to like *cheap* just as much as *pretty* and she painted herself up for the evenings.

The salesmen had got handsy, grabbing at her behind as she stood talking. A lot of men felt they could do that. She tolerated it because there were worse things.

Sean came in quietly. He'd always been a quiet lad until he lost his temper. And even then, he had a tendency to go cold rather than hot. Like her, he'd had to tolerate an awful lot in his youth. Tears or outbursts only got you more of what you didn't want.

"Excuse me," she told the salesmen, from whom she'd been hoping for a fat tip, and abandoned the table.

Sean saw her and smiled. His smiles were a rare thing and, so she'd always thought, changed his face. Cracked it wide open and let out the light.

"Evening, Sean. I'm glad you stopped back." More

than glad.

He glanced around. "Place is busy."

"Don't matter. Sit and have a drink with me. We'll catch up."

"Ain't you supposed to be—uh, working?"

"Entertaining the customers is my job. The customers include you. What'll you have? Beer?"

"Whiskey."

"I'll buy it." She nodded to a table in the corner that had just become available.

"Two whiskeys, Stu," she ordered from the barman. She never drank her allowance of whiskey but always took it.

As she crossed back to the table she eyed Sean and wondered what it was about him. What it had always been. He was no more good-looking than she was pretty. They'd none of them had the kind of upbringing that fleshed a person out and made him or her thrive.

But what Sean had—it was an inward thing rather than an outward one. A kind of strength that even Bennie Clabber's fists hadn't been able to beat down.

She set the drinks on the table and sat opposite him. He inspected her with his quick, pale eyes but didn't comment on the rouge or powder.

"So," she said. "Many people recognize you yet, during your travels around town?"

"Not yet. Haven't been around town much. And I don't suppose folks expect to see the ragged lad from the orphan train back again."

Ireland barely whispered in his voice, more a lingering hint than a presence. He'd been away a long time.

"I'm sure surprised to see you back. You come for

revenge?"

Their eyes met and held. She sensed he thought about denying it, decided he wouldn't. "Yeah."

Sarah made a face. "I'm sure we've all thought about that. Dreamed about it. Except for Rosalee, of course, who was always pampered and petted." Not that Sarah begrudged Rosalee that. They'd all loved her.

Sean's expression softened a mite. "The Thompsons still good to her, are they?"

"Plan on giving her a big, fancy wedding. Wait till you see her. She's so beautiful."

Sean's gaze moved over Sarah's face. He said nothing.

"You remember the Carlsons?" Sarah asked. "Biggest farm in the area. She's marrying their only son, Seth."

"I think I remember seeing him at school. Younger than us. He a good sort?"

"From what I can tell. I expect Rosalee will be all right."

"And what about you, Sarah? From what you said earlier, it sounds like your marriage wasn't—well, an entirely happy one."

She had to think about that, about how to word her reply. "I tend to snipe at Ben a lot, but I'll be honest with you, Sean. It wasn't a love match." How could it have been? "But Milo's right; Ben was a decent enough man, and I decided—"

She'd decided after Sean left town that she'd better settle, if she wanted to survive.

"It was time—past time—to get away from the Gregsons."

"How long were you married?"

"Almost nine years before Ben died. Luke is eight."

"Nearly the age we were when we came out here."

"Yes."

"Your husband, Ben, got killed in an accident? A runaway team, you said."

"Yes. He worked at the livery. Hoped to open his own place someday. Never got the chance. Would have been better if he had. Might have left me with—something."

"Sarah." Sean shifted uncomfortably in his seat. "I hope you won't take this the wrong way, but if you need help…if there's anything I can do—"

There was, but she could hardly ask for that. A man's heart, as she very well knew, was his own. Besides, she barely knew him anymore, not after all this time. All she knew was that the attraction was still there. For her, at least.

She gazed into his pale gray eyes and made a face. "You made it big out west, did you?"

"Big enough. Enough to help a friend." He covered her hand with his where it rested on the table. Warmth flowed through her, a distraction.

Well, what did you know about that? She'd stopped feeling anything when other men touched her. Stopped a long time ago.

"Sarah," he said again. "I hate to think of you—" He paused abruptly. "And with a young son. There must be something else, beyond working here."

"There wasn't, really. After Ben died I tried a few things, but they wouldn't keep me on. We had to eat."

"I get that. The Gregsons wouldn't take you back in?"

"No." She jerked up her chin. "And I wouldn't have

gone even if they'd offered."

"Would have to be better than this."

"Not necessarily." Should she tell him the truth, all of it? This boy turned into a man, who to her had always represented a kind of strength.

No, not yet. Maybe not ever. She hadn't a lot of self-respect. She didn't want to watch the last of it die in Sean Hussey's eyes.

Carefully she withdrew her hand from beneath his. "I'm getting by, Sean. But—thanks for the offer."

"It stands. You need anything—"

"I'll keep that in mind." She changed the subject, saying brightly, "So did you find some place to stay?"

"I did and you'll never believe it." Some strong emotion Sarah couldn't identify moved in his face. "I'm staying with Jenny."

"Jenny."

"And her husband. They have a room to let. Sarah, have you seen her lately?"

Sarah shook her head. "That husband of hers don't like her associating with me. And I don't like to make any trouble for her, 'cause—"

"Her husband beats on her, don't he?"

"I don't know whether he beats on her regular. I'm pretty sure he smacks her from time to time."

"She greeted me with a black eye. Milo wasn't wrong about Cyrus Withers. The man's a bastard."

And there it was. Jenny had all Sean's protective instincts up and ready for a fight.

"Listen," she said as quietly as she could. "Men hit their wives sometimes. Treat them like dirt. I was lucky—Ben never did. Plenty do. And the church says that's all right, it's a husband's duty. You won't do Jenny any favors getting in the middle of that."

"But—"

"Sean, you won't. He'll just take it out on her. It's why I keep away."

She and Jenny Spinner used to be friends. Well, if not friends, at least they understood each other. "You can't do much for a woman in her position, 'cept make it worse."

Sean leaned toward her across the table, an almost frenetic light in his eyes. He lowered his voice to a breathy grunt. "I can, Sarah. I can always kill him."

Chapter Seven

Next morning, Sean rented a horse from the livery with the intention of riding out to the farm. Bennie Clabber's farm where he'd endured five years of servitude.

He'd had very little sleep last night. After he'd returned to the Withers' house and retreated to his room, throwing the window as far open as he could against the stifling heat, he'd heard Jenny and Cyrus arguing. That was, he'd heard Cyrus dressing Jenny down, and her murmured replies.

What he'd heard after that, through the wall that separated the two bedrooms, had been even worse. The creaking of their bed left little doubt what was going on.

In the morning he felt grim and cold-eyed. He wanted to say something to Jenny over the remains of breakfast after Cyrus left for the mill. But Sarah was right. What could he say that wouldn't make Jenny feel worse?

The day at least felt cooler, with a breeze. Rain coming, maybe. He rode the nag he'd hired out slowly along the road from town. He just wanted to get a look at the place where he'd lived. From a distance.

Ten years away and he'd been all over the west. Kansas, Oklahoma, Colorado, Nevada. Even California. He and Billy Dale, after they met up, had followed the trains as long as they needed. After that, in California, he'd acquired a veneer of respectability.

If Billy hadn't fallen in love and got married, they'd probably be doing that yet. Billy falling in love—that had got Sean thinking. About what a man's life could and should hold. About Jenny.

He'd always wondered if she was the one for him. But the odds of him attaining what Billy had found were mighty slim. Only witness the fact that Jenny was already married.

The farm—Clabber's Acres as Bennie had persisted in calling it—came into view, looking so much the same it almost knocked Sean back off his saddle. Same split rail fences, same gently undulating fields. Same cluster of buildings that included the big white house where Sean was so seldom permitted entrance.

There—the pigsties. There the barn where he'd milked the cows. There the wood shed.

A sensation crawled up from Sean's belly, a hot sick one. For an instant he wanted nothing more than to turn his mount around and run, run as he had ten years ago when he was just sixteen.

He'd been big enough by then, if tall and stringy, to hit Bennie back. He'd done so and the resulting answer had been swift and hard. The way Sean saw it then, he had two choices. Run, or stay and die.

He had a third choice now. But he hadn't counted on the strength of his reaction seeing the place, a visceral response that near paralyzed him. He couldn't let his emotions get in the way of this. None of them.

He had a task to accomplish just like when they'd liberated cargo from the trains, as Billy liked to put it. Sean had never let himself think too much about what he did, any more than a man working at a more conventional occupation might. Accomplish the job. Pay Bennie Clabber back as he deserved. Then, as always, away, away.

What about Jenny? Sitting there on the back of his motionless horse, he shook his head. She wasn't his to win. But God, leaving her behind was going to be hard.

He urged the nag into motion and rode on past the farm. It took a while. Bennie had a sizeable spread, which was why he needed cheap labor. Feeding a hand and letting him sleep in the shed he called a bunkhouse cost less than paying a wage.

Sean summoned up a picture of Bennie Clabber. He wasn't a particularly tall man. Sean, who'd done some of his growing after he left here, would now be taller. But he'd had a powerful build, wide shoulders, and plug-like legs bulging with muscle. He could deliver a fearsome blow. Sandy brown hair crawling backward from his forehead and narrow, merciless eyes of light brown.

Sean had upon occasion seen those eyes in nightmares.

He didn't pause when he reached the gate but peered in interestedly. Funny how much the place looked the same. Like barely a day had gone by since Sean left.

He could see a woman hanging laundry out to one side. Would that be Mrs. Clabber or the cook-cum-housekeeper who used to work there? Sean and the other workers had called her Mrs. Sal and if not exactly kind to Sean, she'd been less vicious than Bennie and his wife.

From this distance he couldn't identify the woman. But there was a boy scything grass out farther to the side, having already finished the front. Sean could see the effort it took for him to wield the heavy tool. He had once been that boy.

With a gentle word for the horse, he rode on by and continued far up the road, contemplating his reactions. He'd put a lot of thought into the idea of coming back to settle Bennie. As Billy always said, preparation was half the task.

He couldn't falter now.

The first drops of rain fell as he turned the horse around and rode on back. The boy still swung the scythe. One didn't stop a job until a chore was finished, unless one wanted a swat. But the woman hastily gathered in the sheets she'd just hung on the line.

Sean lowered his hat and encouraged the nag to go faster. After he turned the horse back in at the livery stable, he went to the diner to think things through.

Jenny had worked at this diner when he left. And there she was, back in his head again. A plain-faced girl now took his order, and he sat and eyed the other customers, wondering if he knew any of them.

Nearly five years he'd endured under Bennie Clabber's thumb. It was surprising how little time he'd spent off the farm during that time. There had been school, but Sean—or John as Bennie insisted on calling him—was only allowed to attend when there were no chores on the farm. There were nearly always chores.

They got dragged to church, but Bennie didn't attend there all the time either, citing the demands of the farm. Bennie might bring Sean to the feed store upon occasion to help load an order. But Sean had never been what he'd call a part of the community.

So nobody here looked askance at him. He'd been just another of Bennie Clabber's hands, ten years ago.

The anonymity felt good, after what he'd experienced out at the farm. He relaxed a little and enjoyed the coffee the waitress brought.

The door of the diner opened and three people came in. An older couple with a young woman.

Despite himself, Sean's gaze fixed on the latter. She was small and exquisite with a delicate, somehow exotic face and black hair piled in an elegant upsweep. The couple shepherded her like a favorite chick, and Sean's eyes narrowed.

He didn't recognize her, but after a couple seconds he did recognize the couple. The Thompsons. That meant the exquisite young woman had to be—

Rosalee.

The youngest of them she'd been, that day there on the platform. The day that had changed all their lives. Surely not more than five or six, she'd stood between Jenny and Sarah, still clutching their hands when Bennie Clabber had turned up and dragged Sean away.

While on the train, she'd spent a lot of her time weeping, had Rosalee. She'd tried to cling to Mrs. Kendall but old Kendall would have none of it. Rosalee had barely spoken English then, and had called for her mama in a strange, heartbroken cadence. Both her parents, as Jenny had found out and confided to him, were dead.

A true orphan, unlike Sean. Sean had considered her too young to be sent west, all the same. But the Thompsons had sent a letter—as had all their sponsors—requesting a young girl for their home.

And they'd been good to her, so far as Sean could tell. Treated her like a daughter.

Now the three sat at a table near the front window, Rosalee with her profile toward Sean. He would not have known her. No, he wouldn't. But God, she was pretty.

Dressed like a fine lady of fashion with tiny slippers peeking out from her skirts.

Mr. Thompson ordered tea and cakes. Sean sat and watched. As if his attention alerted her, Rosalee turned her head and met his gaze.

And there he saw the face of the little girl on the platform. Wide, dark eyes. A slightly mournful tilt to the lips. It was her, all right.

Her eyes widened farther and she blinked rapidly. Looked away from him. Spoke to Mrs. Thompson. Engaged in their conversation.

But she kept stealing glances at Sean.

He wondered if she recognized him or something about him.

They were still enjoying their tea when he walked past them without a word, and out into the rain.

Chapter Eight

The rain washed the streets, which was the only good thing Sarah could say about it. The town fathers, including Conrad Clabber who owned the mill, wanted very much for Clabber Mills to be a clean, upstanding town. They regularly instituted initiatives for all the buildings to be freshly painted and what they called beautified.

Any ugly secrets were to be hidden deep.

She half ran to Rachel's house, where her friend quickly let her in. Rachel never asked—because she knew—why Sarah slept till nearly noon or what she'd done at the saloon the night before. Sarah didn't like spending her nights away from Luke, but he was safe housed here. And she earned the money for his board.

It was called survival, and she'd been schooled young in it.

The saloon was no place for Luke. Already at eight she saw signs of rebellion in him. He'd started to complain about having to go to school, and Sarah had no doubt the trouble he and Rachel's boy, Danny, got into with increasing frequency could be laid at Luke's door. Sarah lived in dread that Rachel's husband, Dan, would decide he didn't want Luke staying with them anymore. What she'd do then she could not imagine.

It made her think on Luke's ancestors and what they might have passed down to him. Her own parents had been the kind of people to strike out for the new world without a penny in their pockets. Sarah had always wondered if her pa had been running from something back in Bristol. He'd died in a bar fight not long after they'd reached New York. Her ma had turned to prostitution—setting Sarah a fine example—and perished sometime later from a sickness no one wanted to talk about. Sarah survived in the streets till the Society picked her up.

She'd hoped for good things then. Scary as it was, she'd wanted a better life. What a fool she'd been.

"Sit down," Rachel invited her now, ushering her into the kitchen. "I'll get you some tea."

"Thanks. Where are the boys?"

"Upstairs. Playing at jacks, I think."

Rachel's daughter, Suzie, two years younger than Danny, was rolling out cookie dough at the table. Sarah gave her a smile. "Hello, sweetheart."

"Hello, Aunt Sarah."

She wasn't the girl's aunt, but she and Rachel were close as sisters. Dan and Ben had also been friends.

Ben. She wondered about his people also. Ben had been something of a rolling stone when they met and had turned his hand to any number of things before settling here in Clabber Mills. He'd been quick to stick up for himself and, somewhat like Sarah's own father, not afraid of a fight. If such tendencies did indeed get passed down, she had good reason to fear for Luke.

Not that Ben hadn't there for her, in his way. Sarah had been grateful for him.

Rachel set a teacup in front of Sarah and gave her a searching look. "Rough night?"

"Do I look like I had a rough night?"

"A little bit." Rachel slid into the seat opposite and said carefully, with a glance for Suzie, "You know I worry about you. Your extra duties, so to speak."

"Don't worry about me."

"Can't help it, honey. Those men are drunk. Might do anything."

"Drunk's good. Makes 'em finish faster."

Rachel's cheeks flushed pink. "Honestly, Sarah, I don't know how you can—"

"Not so different from when your husband wants some."

"It is so! That's marriage."

Sarah shrugged. She'd never loved Ben, though she'd appreciated the opportunity he offered her. He'd been a means to get away from the Gregsons when all other means had fallen through. She would have damn near sold her soul for that.

She raised her eyes to Rachel's dark ones. Like her, Rachel wasn't exactly what you'd call a beauty. Also a product of New York's streets, though they hadn't known each other back then, she had buck teeth and an unfortunate jaw. Sarah saw only the kindness in those dark eyes.

"It don't happen often. I don't take many men upstairs. Just when I need—a little extra money. Speaking of which—"

She dug in her purse and piled a handful of coins on the table. Counted it out carefully and put the surplus away. "There's Luke's keep."

Rachel recoiled from the money. "Mercy, Sarah! Did you earn that—"

"Does it matter?"

Rachel gathered up the coins. Sarah smiled at Suzie

again. "What kind of cookies you baking, honey?"

"Ginger snaps."

"Sounds good."

The child went back to her rolling. The two women talked.

"Before I call Luke down to visit, I have to tell you I had a report of him swearing again. Two times. Now I know, Sarah, you don't want him doing that. If you want Dan to strap him—"

"No. I don't." Not to say it mightn't do the boy some good. He was getting mouthy and wild. He needed the example of a man in his life, other than Dan.

But she couldn't bear the thought of her son being punished.

Her thoughts flicked to Sean. Tall and calm and steady. What had put that hard look in his eyes? Was he the kind of man who could put Luke straight?

Who knew what kind of man he was after being away so long? Anyway, such a notion was just a dream like the ones she'd had of Sean before he left Clabber Mills. It had been clear from her conversation with him last night that any interest he possessed rested on Jenny. And what had he done but move right in with the woman?

He'd better be careful. If he showed that interest too much, Cyrus might just kill him for it. Or kill Jenny.

Rachel leaned toward her and asked in a lowered voice, "What is it, honey? What's troubling you?"

Should she confide in her friend? Tell her all of it? She'd never admitted, not even to Rachel, how she felt about Sean or what it had done to her hopes when he'd moved away.

Fact was, not everybody got a happy-ever-after.

She shook her head. "I'm all right. Maybe just a mite tired."

"Things do tend to catch up with us from time to time," Rachel agreed sympathetically.

"That's why I'm grateful to have you, to offer me a cup of tea and a chance to recover some."

"Any time, Sarah."

"Now let me call Luke down here and have a word with him." She wouldn't be able to allow her boy to stay here if he started making trouble for Rachel and Dan. And if she couldn't lodge him here, she had no idea at all what she might do.

There was a big, wide world out there beyond the town of Clabber Mills. But she knew little of it, having lived here from the age of ten. The idea of taking her son and stepping out, trying to survive in that wide world, terrified her.

Some people, like Sean, had the guts to take that kind of step. She was not one of them, having chosen endurance rather than daring.

She walked to the foot of the stairs and hollered for Luke to come down. Both boys came, of course. They were as close as she and Rachel were, which was both a good and a bad thing. Where one went, the other went also.

Which meant Luke could lead Danny right into trouble.

The boys were nearly of a height, Luke maybe an inch or so taller. Both slim and continually outgrowing their clothes. When Luke came clattering down the stairs, he looked so much like Ben, it near squeezed Sarah's heart.

Same dark brown hair that refused to lie flat, always

ruffled. Same narrow, clever face and restless eyes.

Danny's hair was lighter, and he had dark eyes like Rachel's. Otherwise, you might take the two for kin.

"Come into the parlor," Sarah told her son. "I want a few words with you."

Chapter Nine

The parlor felt cool and was rigidly neat. The Everetts rarely used it. Sarah perched on the edge of the stiff sofa and Luke stood in front of her.

Danny had not come in with them, but she had no doubt he lurked outside the door where he could hear everything.

She gazed at her son and he looked back at her. Looking into his eyes felt an awful lot like looking into Ben's.

She still remembered his marriage proposal to her. They'd been seeing each other a while on a limited basis. She had trouble getting away from the farm to see him, but it excited her to do so. She hadn't confided everything to him, not then. But he knew things weren't good for her at the Gregsons' and knew Mrs. Gregson sometimes hit her.

On this particular occasion, she'd had a bruise on her cheek. Ben had scowled at her and asked, "What'd you get that for?"

"Didn't move fast enough. She don't need much reason. Sometimes she thinks I give her lip. I don't." The number of words she'd swallowed rather than spoken fair choked her.

"Well, I reckon you better marry me then and get away out of there."

It hadn't been a romantic proposal, and it had come

out of nowhere. Sarah hadn't expected the half-wild boy she'd been seeing on the sly to prove her salvation.

She didn't love him, no. Couldn't imagine ever loving him. But the offer, offhand as it might be, was a branch extended into the floodwaters of her life.

She'd considered for all of three seconds. Ben had already got handsy with her. He liked to kiss on her and grope her body. She knew if she married him, there would be far more.

It seemed a small price to pay for the miracle of getting away from the Gregsons.

Luke's face came back into focus before her, there in the parlor. He watched her with a combination of defiance and caution it hurt her to see.

Her boy. Ben had been so proud of having a son.

She began in a soft voice, "I hear you've been using curse words. Is it so?"

She hoped he wouldn't lie. In her view, lying and deception were worse than the swearing.

He gave a scant nod.

"Luke, we've talked about this before. I hope you weren't cursing here under this roof?"

"No, Ma. We was playing with some of the boys from school."

"Then how did Aunt Rachel find out about it?" She doubted Danny would tell.

Luke shrugged. "One of the women there doing some cleaning must have heard. Old biddies." The last two words came out sounding so like Ben, she might have smiled had she been less distressed.

"Luke, it's not becoming to swear for any reason. It's not something a gentleman would do."

That made his eyebrows fly up. He wasn't on route

to be a gentleman and neither had his father been.

"I had to swear, Ma."

"Had to?"

"It was either that or pound that ass Jimmy Lester to ribbons along with his gang, and you told me no more fighting."

"Why would you want to pound on Jimmy Lester?"

He pressed his lips tight and just like that, she knew.

"They were talking about me, weren't they?"

He said nothing but, disconcertingly, his eyes filled with tears.

Sarah's throat closed up so she could barely force out the words. "Oh, Luke—"

"He called you a whore. Said you do things—" he stumbled, "do things with men for money. I told him his mother was an ass-lady prig and he was a God-damned liar."

"Luke—"

She should be angry. She knew she should. All she could feel was horror. She grasped hold of him and pulled him into her arms.

For an instant he resisted. Then he wrapped his arms around her fiercely.

"Ma, why do you have to work there? Why can't you work someplace—anyplace—else?"

"That's the job I have, honey, and it keeps us."

He wriggled away from her. "But is it true? What Jimmy said."

"I'm a hostess at the bar, Luke. I serve drinks. Entertain the guests with some conversation."

His dark blue eyes, wise beyond his years, bored into hers. "And go upstairs with them?"

She wiped away the tears that had spilled down his

cheeks. "Don't you worry about that. It's nothing for you to think on." The other boys in town, boys he'd have to attend school with when it started up for the fall term, called her a whore.

"Luke, you listen to me. You're the son of a respectable man"—mostly respectable anyway—"and the woman who was lawfully married to him. You've got nothing to be ashamed of. And if those boys say differently—"

"They did say differently." Luke insisted. "So I swore at them. And I would have pounded Jimmy too, if those ladies hadn't of come running out of the store."

"Fighting," she told him decisively, "fighting's worse than swearing. I'll have none of it."

"Ma, I can't make promises. If they insult you again—"

"Luke, you don't want to grow up into the kind of man who takes care of his problems with his fists. You're better than that."

He looked stubborn. "Maybe I'm not."

"You're a smart boy." God knew, his father had been clever, if devious. "You've got to think of the future ahead of you and the reputation you'll have then. When," she once more struggled for words, "Clabber Mills is far behind us."

He looked surprised and not unpleased. "We leavin'?"

"You may leave some day. To make something fine of yourself." If she had no dreams left for herself, she at least had some for him.

She'd married Ben Rupert when she was barely sixteen. She'd known little else besides this town.

"Meanwhile," she went on in a rush, "You're lucky

to have this place here with Rachel and Dan. I don't want you making things hard for them, understand? And that includes people coming to them telling them you've been swearing."

Luke looked miserable. He said nothing. Despair touched Sarah's heart. Did she have any hope of saving him when she'd been unable to save herself?

Again she thought of Sean Hussey, so miraculously returned. If Sean saved anybody it would be Jenny, not her.

"Run off now and play," she told Luke. "Please be good."

He went. Danny must indeed have been waiting for him outside the door, for she heard two pairs of feet clattering back up the stairs.

Rachel appeared in the parlor doorway. "Did you find out what happened?"

"Boys in town were calling me a whore. Seems he had his choice of swearing or fighting."

"Oh, Sarah."

"He's got it right about those town women—old biddies. They don't think much of me." They hadn't even when she'd been married to Ben. Girl off the train. Low-class scum from the streets of New York. "They'll call Luke for any wrongdoing they can espy."

"Yeah," Rachel agreed. "They always looked down on us, didn't they? Still, Sarah, maybe it's time to try again for other employment. Ask around."

"A job for the woman from the saloon?" Sarah's lips stretched in a tremulous smile. "Is anybody going to hire her to work at a respectable place?"

She'd known when she took the position of hostess at the bar that it would soil her. After getting turned off from the diner, she'd been desperate.

And she'd known better than anyone else she was already as tainted as a girl could be.

Chapter Ten

Sean should have known his first encounter with Bennie Clabber would come unexpectedly. The worst things and less frequently the best things in life always did. Like Bennie Clabber turning up on the platform that day long ago and hauling him away into a life of suffering and misery. Even though he and all the other children had been told they'd be placed with families at the end of their journey, he'd expected—well, something resembling a family rather than sheer servitude.

Over the course of the past ten years, he'd often imagined how his first reacquaintance with Bennie might play out. He pictured himself all grown and well dressed turning up at the man's door. Telling him, when he hauled it open, something along the lines of, *I guess you know why I'm here*, or, *It's time for some payback.*

Over and over again, he'd imagined himself pounding Bennie in the face until he bled and cried for mercy, or holding him at gunpoint. Hearing that limp rag of a wife of his screech and wail.

The thing he hadn't reckoned with in all that time was the notion of Bennie forgetting him. Though he'd carried Bennie in his thoughts all the while, the man had dismissed one scrap of humanity he'd called John Hussey from his.

Hatred, or so it seemed, lasted longer than disparagement.

He and the others brought in to work the farm, be they hired or taken in like Sean, were no more important than the animals that were born and eventually slaughtered on the land.

He left Jenny's house early the next morning, following another night of listening to the bed creak in the room next door. Cyrus rode his wife hard and Sean could only wonder what was in her mind. How did it feel to be struck by the man who was meant to love and protect you, and then forced to accommodate him?

In order to avoid the temptation of asking her, he cleared out before his breakfast, which he got at the diner in town. As he ate, he watched the streets fill up—busy this morning, and a lot of people gathered down at the stock pens, past the train station. Must be auction day.

He remembered past auction days quite vividly. Watching Bennie Clabber jockey and scheme to get the best prices and stock to improve his herds. Sean had always pitied the critters who came under Bennie's so-called care.

Bennie cared about the best deal. The bottom line. Nothing more.

After Sean finished his breakfast, he started down to where the commotion was centered. To his surprise he saw Phil Phillips, the same auctioneer who'd served when he'd last been in town. Dozens of farmers and hands stood around waiting for the sale to begin. Cattle lowed pitifully from the pens.

He didn't want to stay and watch, but the spectacle caught him and he lingered. Three animals were sold and carted off in quick succession before he turned and saw two men standing together at the far side of the crowd.

Bennie Clabber and his brother Conrad, who owned

Clabber Mills.

The shock of it went through Sean like a bullet and tore him up like one. If he'd thought his reaction to riding out and seeing the farm had been bad, this dwarfed it. He went hot all over and began to shake. Even though—

Standing there in the hot sunshine, which had resumed after yesterday's rain, he was also aware of surprise. From his new perspective, that of a man twenty-six years old, Bennie did not look quite so intimidating. Nor did his brother, the biggest employer and the most important man in town. Just two men. Not that tall. Not that strong. Only men.

Knowing that did nothing for Sean's emotional state. He had to draw quick breaths and steady himself. Had to discipline the desire to get away.

And then, just as if Sean's gaze drew Bennie's attention, the man looked over at him, and their eyes locked there amid the crowd.

Bennie did not recognize him. That much was clear from the flat expression in his eyes and the way his gaze then slid on past Sean without much interest.

But it returned again. Must wonder why I'm staring at him. But you'd think he'd remember the boy he bullied for almost five years.

Bennie said something to his brother, who also glanced in Sean's direction. Sean tugged the brim of his hat down and stepped back out of sight.

No, this wasn't the way he'd wanted it to go. He'd wanted to be bold and assertive, to push Bennie's past cruelties back in his face. To be the fearless man he'd become.

Instead he felt near as sick and weak as the boy who'd been dragged away from the train station that day with a swat to the head.

Blundering off in the direction of the saloon—if he'd ever needed a drink it was now—he bumped into someone.

"Sean? You all right?"

Milo stood there with the lead of a calf in his hand, and a concerned look in his brown eyes.

"No, Digger, I don't suppose I am. I've just seen Bennie Clabber."

Milo's gaze quickened with understanding. "Seen him? As in, had words?"

"No." Sean shook his head. "It didn't take that to rattle me."

"Jesus, Sean. You're white as a ghost."

"Funny thing is, I don't think he recognized me." If anyone would understand, it would be Milo.

"Well, you do look a mite different with the hat and the fine clothes. And I don't expect he ever thought to see you again."

"No."

"You need a drink. I'd go over with you, but I have to get this calf home."

Home. Had either of them ever had one?

"A bit early for a drink, ain't it?" he asked even though he agreed with Milo's opinion. "Jesus, Milo. How'm I ever gonna face the man down if I can't even look at him?"

A wise expression came to Milo's eyes. "You're strong, Sean. God knows, we all are. Otherwise we'd never have survived what we been through."

Sean supposed the train to nowhere had given them that.

"I ain't used to feeling that way anymore. Scared

and intimidated."

"No, I reckon you ain't." Milo reached out and clasped Sean's shoulder. "Give yourself some time, hear? You came back to face him down, right? You'll do just that."

Sean nodded. What he wanted to do was beat Bennie Clabber senseless, put him on the receiving end of the feeling he'd just experienced.

"You're right. There's no timeline for this. He'll get what he has coming when he gets it."

Milo nodded. "Just hope I'm there to see, is all."

****

Since Sean's self-respect wouldn't allow him to take refuge at the saloon so early in the day, he walked back to Jenny's instead. The tiny house stood quiet when he arrived, Cyrus long gone to work, and he paused with one foot on the porch steps, something in the garden catching his eye.

A blade of grass here. He stooped down and plucked it out. A weed there, a little farther along. Before he knew it, he was on his knees dirtying up his good trousers as he weeded the patch of ground Jenny had neglected.

"What are you doing?"

He hadn't heard her come out, but she stood on the porch above him.

"Just weeding these few spots you missed."

"I was going to get to that after I finished hanging the laundry."

He looked up at her. Their gazes met and held. "You don't have to make any excuses to me, Jenny."

She puffed out a breath. "You're wrong, Sean. Seems I have to make excuses to everybody. To Cyrus for—for everything. Cyrus's ma back in Pittsburgh for not having given her a grandchild yet. Ain't like we're not trying—"

After only two nights, Sean could testify to that. He got to his feet, the weeds in his hands.

"Didn't mean to upset you, Jenny. I just didn't want you to get in trouble if you forgot this little task."

"You shouldn't have to follow after me doing my chores."

"Lord, Jenny. Do you know how many weeds I've pulled in my day? Acres of them."

All at once she was weeping, her hands pressed to her face. Sean stood there aching to take her in his arms, knowing he couldn't.

"Honey, I didn't mean to make you cry."

"I hardly ever cry. Gave it up a long time ago. It's just that I'm not used to somebody looking after me."

He wanted to look after her. Wanted it more than anything—almost.

He wanted to settle Bennie Clabber even more.

"Let's go inside. Talk a while. Nobody here to bother us now."

She gave him a doubtful look from out of her bruised face. "It would be nice—nice to have somebody to talk to."

"Then I'm your man."

If only he was.

Chapter Eleven

"Remember that first day when the train stopped at Clabber Mills? When we all stood there on the platform?" Jenny had made tea and seemed to have regained some of her composure while sitting with Sean at the kitchen table.

"I surely do," he told her.

"My knees were knocking so hard I thought I'd fall down. I stood there holding poor little Rosalee's hand on one side and Digger's on the other. And that horrible woman—"

"Mrs. Kendall."

"Yes. She hadn't a drop of pity in her, did she? I mean, Rosalee hadn't stopped crying for her mama all the way out, and all that woman did was tell her to be quiet."

"I saw her. I saw Rosalee in the café with Mr. and Mrs. Thompson. She looked—"

"Beautiful?" Jenny finished for him with a tight smile. "She is beautiful. And about to make a fortunate marriage. I hear her wedding's going to be a grand occasion."

"The whole town going to be attending?"

"Most of it." Jenny made a face. "I'm not invited."

"How come most of us off the orphan train weren't considered quite respectable but Rosalee's wedding is an event?" Sean asked almost rhetorically.

Jenny answered sourly. "I think it's because the Thompsons always treated her like their own daughter, different from the rest of us. Mrs. Thompson always wanted a little girl, and she took Rosalee straight to her heart. She was so small when we came here. So pretty."

You're pretty. Sean didn't say that aloud, though he thought it. There was just something about Jenny that had always pulled at him. Pretty curls. Pretty brown eyes. Pretty bruised face.

With a sudden rush, he wanted to kill Cyrus Withers.

"I imagine," Jenny said, seemingly in the mood now to talk, "that's the way the folks at the Society back in New York hoped all our sponsors would be. Like Rosalee's, I mean. They couldn't otherwise have been so cruel as to send us to the fates we actually got."

"People like Mrs. Kendall and the other escorts had to know." Mrs. Kendall had seen Bennie Clabber whack Sean in the head, there at the station. She hadn't lifted a finger to intervene.

"Maybe they get hardened to it, Sean, after a while."

"I expect so."

"Anyway, what I want to say is, I'm real grateful for your kindness. It's a wonder you have any in you either, after what you've been through. But I don't want you getting mixed up between me and Cyrus, understand? You've got to leave my chores for me to do."

Chores. Just like when they were small. Was she the man's wife, or his servant? His whore, at night.

He asked bitterly, "So he can find fault and hit you again?"

Her gaze fell. "Cyrus is a right particular sort of man. Likes things done a certain way. Us not having a baby yet is a sore disappointment to him. I keep failing him, you see, in all I try to do."

"That don't give him the right, Jenny, to hurt you."

"Well, it does and it doesn't. Just—it won't do any good for you to try and get in the way. It'll just make him angrier."

It struck Sean that a woman shouldn't have to fear her husband's moods, or his anger.

"You see," Jenny slid forward slightly on her chair and addressed Sean earnestly. "I didn't think anyone would ever propose to me, the drudge who worked at the diner. When Cyrus took an interest and started coming in to see me—well, it seemed like a miracle. A chance to escape. I guess I didn't look at him too hard before I leaped."

He should have stuck around, Sean thought for the first time ever. Sure, leaving Clabber Mills had been the best choice for him. But if he'd stuck around for a few more years, taken the punishment and the insults Bennie handed out, he might have been the one to propose to Jenny. To save her.

Surely he could have endured some more mistreatment for the sake of that?

An instant later, he realized the truth. If he'd stayed, he'd never have been in a position to propose to Jenny anyway. No home, no earnings to save up. If he'd waited till he was grown, he might have found a job in town and earned those things.

Lawfully.

But who would have given him a job? Conrad Clabber never would have agreed to take him on at the mill. And Conrad Clabber more or less controlled the town.

Still, he should have stayed. Been the one to rescue

Jenny, maybe win her heart. As it was, he'd arrived too late.

"That how you met him, Cyrus? At the diner?"

"I saw him there, yes. But the first time he showed any real interest was at a dance." Her face didn't light over the memory as it should. "A summer dance. I never went to those things. Not sure why I went that time. To listen to the music, maybe. I didn't do any dancing. I couldn't dance. But he noticed me. Asked me." Jenny swept Sean with a look. "Nobody had ever noticed me."

I had. Sean ached to say the words. He didn't.

"You could leave him, you know."

"What?" She actually gasped.

"If he's mean to you, keeps on hitting you and making you do things you don't want to—"

"I couldn't! He's my husband. And—and it's not all bad. I have a home of my own, don't I? And for a girl off the train, that's simply miraculous."

Sean felt like a knife had pierced his heart. Did she want to stay with Cyrus?

"I just have to be sure and fulfill all my duties and it will be fine."

"Well if I catch him hitting you again, if it happens while I'm here, he and I are gonna have a problem. Right?"

"Sean, please don't interfere."

"Jenny, you can't expect me to just stand by—"

"You'd make it so much worse. I understand you feel—well, something like a big brother to me. We five who got off the train together are the closest we have to family. And I'm grateful. But...well..." her eyes beseeched him, "I've made my bed."

And he'd come back too late.

He nodded, though it went hard with him. "If you ever need anything like money, well, I have a bit put aside from—from workin' out west. It's yours for the asking."

Tears came to her eyes again. "That's good of you."

"If you do ever decide to leave him, I could pay for your fare. You could get back on that train—"

"And go where?"

"Anywhere."

"I don't know anyone back in New York, not any more. I'd be lost."

"Just keep it in mind, Jenny. You've got a way out if you need it."

"Thank you, Sean." She picked up her teacup, which rattled a little against the saucer. "Now tell me all about your time away. What sort of work did you do, that brought you so much prosperity?"

Sean sat and spun her some lies till she realized it grew late and ran out back to tend the laundry. He went up to his stuffy room and changed his clothing. By the time he came down again, the wash was all in and neatly folded. Supper simmered on the stove, and Cyrus Withers was just arriving home from his day at the mill.

"Supper will be on the table straightway, Mr. Hussey," Cyrus greeted him. "You know, I been asking around town about you. You were one of them hands out at Bennie Clabber's farm."

"That's right."

"Right rebellious, so Mr. Clabber said. Says you gave his brother no end of trouble before you run off."

"That's right." Ah, so Conrad Clabber did remember him. He stared Cyrus in the eye. "Came a time I got big enough to stop taking guff from anyone."

Cyrus flushed ruddily. "I thought you were a legitimate businessman. Not sure I should let you stay here now."

"I am a legitimate businessman. Here to take care of some things."

"Came back to gloat, most likely." Cyrus's gaze slipped over Sean's fine suit.

"Not a man for gloating, me."

"Cyrus," Jenny had come up beside them. "Supper's ready."

"Well, all right." Cyrus stretched to his full height. "We'll go in to the table."

Suddenly Sean knew he couldn't sit there with the two of them. "Sorry, Jenny, to miss your fine cooking, but I'm going to town."

Cyrus bristled. "Meals come included with your board."

"I understand that. Ain't too hungry."

"I ain't giving any of your board back."

"Wouldn't dream of asking you to." Sean marched out of the tiny white house, leaving the two of them alone.

Chapter Twelve

The farmhand sitting at the table in the corner was grabby, as Sarah had found out the hard way when she took his and his companions' drinks over to them. Three men, there were, and they must have just got paid because they looked ready to throw their money around.

The young one with the brown hair had pinched her backside right through her skirt and petticoat and made it pretty clear what he wanted. He'd ask her about going upstairs before long. She'd better make up her mind what she wanted to do about it.

Her criteria for whom she would and wouldn't take upstairs was not too narrow. What he looked like didn't really matter because she kept her eyes tight shut the whole time. In this case he wasn't a bad-looking boy. And he appeared like he'd washed today, which was a plus, as was his youth. The older the man, the harder he tried to work at it. These young boys went off right quick and were done.

All in all, she figured she'd wind up taking him. Luke needed a pair of shoes—again—and that meant she needed the money.

Fact was, she'd dressed herself up this evening for just that purpose. Put on her most revealing dress and swept her hair up all fancy. Tucked a glittery comb there, the one Ben had given her on their first anniversary.

The barman, Stu gave her a look and jerked his head

toward the farmhand. She crossed over to talk to him.

"Looks like you got a customer," he said. "You takin' him up?"

"In a while. Maybe." The owner, Mr. Bracer, never pushed her to accept customers, but when she did, Stu had instructions to pay attention so he could take the boss's cut. "I'll let him get a little drunker first."

"Right. I'll keep the drinks coming."

The door opened and Sean Hussey came in. Tall and quiet, he stood for an instant as if studying the room, and Sarah's whole body came to attention. It was as if she went from half-slumber to awakening.

Stu glanced at her. "He was in here before, wasn't he? Who is that?"

"Customer." And a friend.

She sent Sean a smile, and he crossed over to the bar.

"Two whiskeys," Sarah ordered before Sean could speak. "Put mine on my tab."

To Sean she said, "Good evening, Sean."

"Sarah."

"Don't you look all gussied up?" He looked good enough to eat.

Surprise flitted across his face. "Wanted to get out of the Withers house for a while."

"Good. Let's sit and have a drink."

The farmhand across the room forgotten, she led Sean to a table in the corner. Stu brought the two whiskeys and slapped them down.

Sarah feasted her eyes on the man across from her. The dark blue suit hadn't come cheap, and he'd put on his hat at a rakish angle. His pale gray eyes, still watchful, studied the room over her shoulder. "Busy tonight."

"I think some of the hands got paid."

The gray eyes moved to her face. "That mean you'll be busy too?"

"It's all right. I'm free to entertain who I like."

"Entertain." He made a face.

"Yeah." She said it softly. Would he come upstairs with her if she asked? Lord have mercy, only imagine. Sean Hussey hers for the night. She could strip those fine clothes from him. A heady dream come true.

The thought shocked her, though. She hadn't wanted anything in so long, she barely recognized the impulse for what it was.

"Couldn't abide staying at the Withers' and watching Cyrus abuse Jenny any longer." He drank from his whiskey.

Well, there was a reminder of just where Sean's interest lay. Sarah managed another smile. "Consider this your home away from home, any time you need a refuge."

"Never had a refuge." He drank again and she signaled Stu for another drink. Maybe if Sean got drunk enough, he'd forget she was Sarah and not Jenny.

They talked for a while about the changes in the town, and Sean worked on his second drink.

All of a sudden he nodded at the glass in front of her. "Why d'you do that?"

"Do what?"

"Order a drink and just let it sit? You did the same before."

"I get my drinks for free."

"But you don't drink 'em. Why?"

"Want to know the truth?"

His light eyes fastened on her face. "Always."

"I'm afraid if I start drinking I won't be able to stop, and then the boogie-men from the past will swoop in and get me."

"Boogie-men?"

"There's not much keeping them at bay. Just these walls I've put up and have to kind of keep in place. If I get tipsy, those walls might fall down."

He studied her seriously. "Describe these boogie-men to me."

She didn't want to. "Can't. That might invite them in."

He drew a breath and covered her hand with his where it rested on the table. "Honey—"

"No, Sean. I dare not let 'em in."

"All right, then. I won't ask nothing more."

"They're—they're like the ones you see in nightmares."

He shook his head. "I don't dream much anymore. Used to when we first came here. I used to dream I was back in New York. Running the streets. Looking for my ma."

"But she died on the way over from Ireland, right?"

"Fancy you remembering that."

She remembered everything about him.

"Never looked for my pa. Knew where to find him. In a pub. With a glass." He looked down at his own drink as if startled.

"Right now," she confided, "I'm living my life for my boy, Luke. All I do is for him."

"Not for yourself?"

"No."

"You wanting nothing for yourself—"

Oh, she wanted.

"—don't seem fair."

"Were you happy out west, Sean?"

He shrugged uncomfortably. "I don't think *happy* described my state of mind. There were moments when I felt pretty good."

"Never married?"

"Nah."

"Never tempted?"

He shook his head.

So he was free. And she was free. For an instant Sarah caught a glimpse of something so wonderful, it dazzled her mind's eye. He, though, was interested in Jenny, who wasn't free.

Sean peered over her shoulder. "There's a young man on the other side of the room watching you. Glaring at me as if he wants to punch holes in my head."

"Oh, that's a boy in from the farm. He thought he was going upstairs with me, before you came in."

"And is he? Going upstairs with you?"

"Not sure."

Sean drained his second whiskey. "Sarah, how can you do it? That?"

Surprised by the question from him, a man of the world, so to speak, she hesitated. "Why, I just sort of switch my mind off."

"You can do that?"

"Yeah."

"Damn."

She pushed her whiskey at him. He picked it up and drank.

"You shouldn't have to—" He clapped the glass down. "Hold on. Here he comes."

Sarah peered over her shoulder. Sure enough, the

farm hand—a big, husky youth—was on his way to their table with a scowl on his face.

After a scathing look, he focused just a bit blearily on Sarah. "Come on. We goin' upstairs."

"Mister, I think you misunderstood. I never agreed—"

"I didn't misunderstand nothin'. We had us an un-unspoken agreement."

He was right, they had, more or less. Maybe she should excuse herself from the table and take him upstairs. Because Stu was watching and—

"Perhaps," Sean said, "the lady has changed her mind."

The farmhand focused on him. "You think you can waltz in here and snatch her away? I saw her first and she's mine tonight."

Sean got to his feet. He'd downed the better part of three whiskeys in quick succession but he looked cool and steady, with danger in those light eyes.

"The lady ain't something to be bargained over, boy. She's—"

"Stop callin' her a lady, you damn fool. She's a whore and she's comin' with me."

The farmhand seized Sarah's arm and yanked her up from the table. The whole room now watched, and Stu had started forward from behind the bar.

Sean struck so quickly, Sarah never saw the blow. She heard it, though, when Sean's fist connected with the farmhand's jaw. The boy staggered but didn't go down— he was a big lad. Neither did he let go of Sarah's arm.

"Get your hands off her." It came in a growl as Sean leaped across the table, which promptly collapsed. From the corner of her eye, Sarah saw Stu go back and grab the shotgun from behind the bar.

The farmhand struck back at Sean, launching a flurry of blows. A roundhouse punch missed its target and hit Sarah instead, high on the cheekbone.

She sat down abruptly on the rather sticky floor and the bar went silent.

"God damn it!" Sean growled. Sarah looked up at him—all coiled fury. His hat had fallen off and his sandy hair was ruffled. She'd never seen anyone look so dangerous.

"Sarah?" Stu yelped. "You all right?"

Dead silence met the query.

After a minute, Sarah broke it. "I'm fine. I think."

Sean stood up to the farmhand, who now looked mightily chagrined. "Big man, hitting a woman. Ain't nothing lower on God's earth."

"I didn't mean to hit her. She got in the way—"

Sarah climbed to her feet with Stu's help. Her cheek still stung and her head felt a little woozy, but she didn't want any more trouble.

The farmhand looked at her pitifully. "You still goin' upstairs with me?"

Sarah glanced at Stu.

It was Sean who answered. "No, she ain't. She's going upstairs with me tonight."

What?

The farmhand slunk away to his companions. Sarah stood there with her head spinning, and Sean put his arm around her.

"You sure you're all right? Don't need to see a doctor or anything?"

Was she all right? "I don't need a doctor."

Sean glanced at the barman. "Her shift's done,

understand?"

"Yes, sir."

"Sarah, how much is it?"

"What?"

"How much does it cost to take you upstairs?"

She whispered, ashamed, "A dollar."

Sean fished in his pocket and slapped a dollar in Stu's palm.

"There. I'm sure that fulfills your obligations."

Chapter Thirteen

At the top of the stairs, Sarah swayed and turned toward her rescuer. Sean.

"Here." He still had his arm around her. "You sure you're not gonna faint on me?"

"It was just a glancing blow."

"Enough to knock you down."

"Listen, Sean." She fixed her gaze on his face. "You don't have to do this. Come into the room with me, I mean."

"Sure I do."

Her heart leaped, but he went on, "How will it look if I come down right away? I'll stay the night. Make sure nobody sneaks up and bothers you. I don't trust that barman."

"What are you, a—a knight in shining armor?"

"Hardly. Let's get you inside so you can lie down. Which room?"

"This one."

She wanted to lie down. What was more, she wanted to lie down with Sean. And that, quite simply, had never happened to her before, not even with Ben.

There'd always been tolerance. Endurance. No desire.

In the room, she turned again to face him. This was a barren little place, and she felt ashamed to show it to him. She made no move for the light.

"Steady," he murmured and took her in his arms, wrapping both of them around her this time. She could feel him and smell him—a clean, beguiling scent—and warmth crept through her, far more disorienting than the blow to the face.

She leaned into that warmth the way a plant might. One that desperately needed the sun to survive. She couldn't see his face in the dark. She didn't need to.

His breath gusted across her cheek and her heartbeat accelerated. Their lips were only inches apart. Did she dare? Did she dare reach up and press her mouth to his?

She never kissed men. She let those she chose to bring up here slobber on her, paw at her, pound on her, but she didn't invite anything save with the practiced words, "So what can I do with you tonight?"

Now she had no words. They'd all been stopped by the flood of desire.

She went up on her tiptoes and pressed her lips to Sean's.

He tasted like the whiskey he'd consumed and somehow like the way he smelled. She'd never tasted anything better and it went straight to her head.

He stiffened, and for one terrible moment she thought he would pull away. They seemed to teeter together on a precipice before he gusted her name into her mouth.

"Sarah."

And fell into the kiss.

Sarah quite clearly felt him succumb. Still on her tiptoes, she twined her arms around his neck and pulled his head down to hers.

How many years had she imagined kissing Sean Hussey? How long had she regretted never doing this before he left town? Now it was better, better than she could have dreamed. It lit her up inside and rendered her helpless. For these few moments there was only him and her, and the dark air of the room as the world fell away.

When he broke the kiss, she moaned in protest. He touched his forehead to hers and said, "Sarah—I didn't mean…I didn't come up here to—"

"Don't you want to?" Was that her voice? Husky with desire.

"Didn't say that." He trapped her face between the palms of his hands with exquisite gentleness. This time he kissed her, a deep kiss that, yes, tasted of desire. When the kiss ended, he drew her close against him and she could feel he was hard and ready for her.

"Sarah, I came up here to protect you, not take advantage."

"I know." Blindly she reached for his mouth again, hoping her kiss would say what she could not. She wanted this. For the first time in her life, she might have something she wanted desperately. "Come on. Come to the bed."

Would he have done as she asked if he hadn't had three whiskeys? She would never know. At that moment, standing on unfamiliar ground, she dismissed the question. Poised there beside the bed, she helped him off with his coat and turned back the covers before she started working on the buttons of her dress, fumbling.

"Here. Let me."

His fingers moved nimbly despite the drink. She stood while he stripped her naked and even that didn't feel like anything that had ever happened to her before, because he did it with such care.

When she stood there bare—revealed to him—he

kissed her again and she started on the buttons of his shirt.

Warm, supple skin met her fingers. He didn't have a lot of hair like some men. Just hard muscle, a quiet strength that made her knees give way.

He swung her onto the bed. Stood there for a moment regarding her.

How much could he see in the dark? The marks left on her belly after she'd carried Luke? A couple bruises from where the last man she'd invited up here got a little rough?

Don't think about that. This is Sean. This is new.

He shed the last of his clothes and crawled onto the bed on top of her.

"Sarah—" he began again.

"Don't talk." To keep him from it she wrapped her arms around him and kissed him again. His weight settled between her thighs and she braced herself. This was the moment when most men went at it.

Sean didn't. Instead, with his mouth still fastened to hers, he began to touch her. His hand moved first to one breast, cupping, caressing. His palm abraded her nipple before he broke the kiss to bend his head and suckle her.

Desire swamped her, overcame her just like a raging prairie fire. She lay there with him gathered to her breasts, the hot weight of him pressed between her thighs, and ruffled his hair, knowing she'd do anything for this man. Give him whatever he asked.

"Don't stop," she begged when he lifted his head from her breast to look into her face. But he only kissed her again and his hand moved between their bodies. His fingers entered her, entered her below like a whisper of magic.

She arched her body and opened to him.

Open your legs to me. That was what Mr. Gregson used to say when he came to her room after dark. *Stupid wench. That's all you're good for*.

Even that memory couldn't ruin this moment, when Sean put his fingers inside her and all her desire coiled tight before bursting and blossoming into love for him.

Did love make the difference? Was that the magic that turned pain into pure pleasure?

Not till he had her flowing like a river did he slip inside, and they moved together, moved and moved till the pleasure became unbearable again, and they rocked and shattered as one. She lay then clutching him, clutching him hard, the smooth expanse of his back beneath her fingers.

Holding him to her heart.

She wanted to weep. And she wanted to tell him all kinds of things she shouldn't. A woman had to protect herself. That was one lesson she'd learned early and learned well.

He'd completely undone her, had Sean Hussey. At least she thought she was already undone before he stirred and whispered in her ear, "Sarah, darlin'? You all right?"

The softness of Ireland filled his voice. What they'd done together seemed to have brought back the Irish of his youth, though this was no boy she held in her arms.

"Yes. Sean?" She probably shouldn't tell him how long she'd wanted this. Wanted him. That she'd admired him ever since that terrible day they'd stood on the platform together. That what he'd just given her was far better than any imagining.

"Um?" He settled down next to her, his head finding

her pillow, one arm and one leg still flung over her. She could spend the rest of her life this way and complain of nothing.

"I want you to know that wasn't because you paid a dollar." The last thing she wanted was for him to think of her as a whore. When the buzz from the whiskey wore off, she didn't want him regretting this.

When he remembered Jenny.

"I did this—I did it because I wanted to." And that was as close as she could get to telling him what was in her heart.

"That's good, honey." He sounded drowsy. The effects of the whiskey, no doubt. Or their great shared expenditure of energy. "Sleep," he told her, and stroked her face.

Because she could deny him nothing ever again, she did.

Chapter Fourteen

Sean woke by inches and lay wondering where he was. In the past, he'd awakened in all kinds of places. Strange rooms, and stables, and out on the prairie. In the desert. Alone or with someone else.

Usually he snapped awake all at once, senses on alert for danger. Not like this.

An unfamiliar room with daylight creeping in the single window. He lay in a bed and not alone, because he could feel warmth beside him.

A woman.

He'd had one hell of a dream. One of those that came to him only seldom. For him, having sex was just that, a body function that satisfied a need. This had been different. In the dream, he'd made love.

Twice.

They'd moved together in the dark, as if being so close together they couldn't do anything else. It had been blindingly, blisteringly good.

Had it actually happened? Had he just dreamed it? Swiftly he took stock of himself. Naked between a pair of rough sheets. Body spent. By God—

He raised up on one elbow and looked narrow-eyed at the woman beside him. Light brown hair tumbled from an upsweep she'd failed to take down. A slender curve of naked shoulder. A bruised cheek.

Sarah.

Memory slammed into him then like a freight train. He relived it all. Coming up here with her last night. Wanting to protect her from what had happened downstairs. Kissing and catching fire. Rocking together in the bed on a rush that allowed for no thought.

Had the rest of it been a dream? Or had they moved together again during the night?

Sarah. What had he been thinking?

She still slept, her face turned away from him and the bruised cheek upward. A good thing she still slept, because it would be awkward as hell when she woke up.

Still and all, that had been the best damn sex he'd ever had.

He lay there studying the ceiling over his head and tried to figure out why. True, it had been a while since he'd lain with anyone. He'd been primed, so to speak. But it wasn't just that.

Something about the way she'd touched him. The way she'd felt when he touched her. The taste of her when they kissed. The way she'd responded when he touched her breasts.

God damn it, he was ready for her again. And that— well, it wasn't even decent.

Sarah—Sarah was one of his own. Part of the little family of five who had stood together on the train platform. He never wanted to hurt her in any way. Didn't want her to think he'd used her.

Because she was Sarah, and despite the things she had to do to support herself and her boy she was decent to the core. A young girl who had been pushed. Just because they'd moved together between the sheets—

"Morning."

She'd opened her eyes and lay watching him quietly,

her expression unreadable. Was she embarrassed? He had to admit, that emotion contributed to the others that filled him.

"Morning, honey. How you feeling? How's that cheek?"

She brushed her fingers across it. "Sore. I must be a sight."

She was. Parts of her hair were still pinned up. The rest straggled onto the pillow. Sean had plunged his fingers into that hair last night while they kissed. And kissed.

Sarah had a plain face, all except for her eyes, which were beautiful. She'd painted that face up last night. It looked a bit tawdry in the morning light.

He tried to summon up a smile, to act as if this was ordinary, but it wasn't. He was pretty sure she was still naked under the blankets. Warm and soft. And him still at half-mast. Who'd have thought he could feel so much lust for Sarah, of all women? His friend.

She sat up, and the blanket tumbled. She caught it just before it revealed her breasts. Lovely breasts.

"Sean, I hope you don't think—well, what could you think? You know that I bring men up here sometimes. I don't want you to think I did this for the money."

"Yeah, you said that last night." It had all come back to him now. Every touch. Each kiss.

"What we shared last night, Sean, it wasn't like any other time. Not for me."

"For me, either."

Her face lit. "Truly?"

"Sarah, honey, you mind if I ask you something?"

Her expression turned guarded, but she said, "Sure,

Sean. Go ahead."

"How can you—well, what I mean to say is, I know you. I've known you since we landed in Clabber Mills together. And us knowing each other and being friends, I'm sure that made a difference in what we—uh—shared last night."

"I suppose so."

"But how d'you do it with strangers? Bring 'em up here and—"

Emotions flickered in her eyes and Sean wondered if he'd offended her. Maybe he should have kept the question to himself. But they couldn't be much closer than they were right now. And the matter troubled him.

"I don't bring men up here often. Not as often as you might think. When I do—well, it's the way I told you last night. There's a sort of door in my mind and I can slam it shut. It's like I remove myself from what's going on till it's over. It usually doesn't take long. And it's just my body, see? And the truth is, it's all I'm fit for."

"Sarah! Why would you say something like that?"

"Because it's true."

"It isn't."

Her gaze dropped abruptly. "It's what Mr. Gregson used to say."

"What?"

"When he'd come to my room. Back at the farm." She clutched the blanket to her chest and gazed at him while horror at her words crawled up from his belly and over his skin.

"You mean—"

"He'd come to my room. Late at night. Force himself on me."

"Rape you, you mean?"

Sarah nodded soberly.

"When? For how long?"

"It started not long after we got here. Kept up till I got away, married Ben. That was after you left town."

"Why didn't you tell anyone?"

Helplessly, she shook her head. "He made me feel so dirty. Said if I told, everyone would know it was my fault. That it was all I was good for—"

"Stop saying that! You should have told me."

"Yes? And what could you have done? You were a boy getting beat on regular by Mr. Clabber. Anyway, it was my secret. I didn't tell anyone, ever, except my friend Rachel."

"Sarah—"

"When Ben asked me to marry him, it was a miracle. It meant I could get away. But Ben—well, he wanted the same thing Mr. Gregson had, and that was hard for me. I found out I could shut the door with Ben too. Just—just let it happen. But, Sean," she touched his hand, "I want you to know it wasn't like that with you." Her gaze beseeched him. "I stayed with you the whole time we did what we did last night. I experienced it all. I'm not sure what made the difference, but—it was like nothing else I've ever known."

"It was good for me too, Sarah. Real good."

"I don't want you to think of me as just a—a woman who sells her body."

"I don't, honey. I can't believe what you've endured—"

"It's just…I don't have much else to sell, with Ben gone and Luke to raise. I'm not good for—"

He laid his finger against her lips. "Don't say it, Sarah. Don't ever say that again. Listen to me. I don't want you to ever be with any man again, unless you want to. You're worth more than that. So much more."

"Am I, though? We were nothing but rats from the streets—"

"We were. No longer." His blood fairly boiled at what that devil Gregson had done to her. He wanted to travel straight out to the Gregson farm and settle that bastard as he deserved. Why, Sarah couldn't have been more than ten or eleven when they'd got here. He shuddered at the very idea.

"People might have treated us like we were scum, but no more. You've got somebody to help you now. A friend."

"A friend." She repeated it a bit weakly.

"Sure thing. I've got some money. I'll set you up out of this place. Help you along till you get a better job."

"Doing what?"

"You learned a lot on the farm, more than what— what that bastard taught you." Not that Sean didn't understand. There had been times while Bennie Clabber was beating on him, his mind had kind of gone away like that. So he wouldn't feel the hurt. And the shame. God, Sarah must be carrying such a load of shame.

Her gaze searched his. "You planning to stay here in Clabber Mills?"

"No." He'd come back to settle Bennie, had added Cyrus to his list. Seemed like he had a third debt to settle now.

"But, honey, I can set you up as I say, and see you safe before I leave. Right?"

He did not understand, quite, the grief that came to her eyes. He fought it by telling her, "You'll never have to do this again, Sarah. I promise."

He would create some good, he vowed to himself, from the harm that had been done.

Chapter Fifteen

After Sean left, once he'd climbed back into his clothes and slipped from the room like a shadow, Sarah wept.

She lay in the bed and sobbed into her pillow the way she hadn't since those first days after she'd arrived in Clabber Mills. Since before she'd learned that tears didn't do any good. That crying only made you feel sick and stuffy in the head, on top of helpless.

Now she wept because she'd fallen from such a height. From the peak she'd reached in Sean's arms right back into the mire that was her life.

She'd confided her secret, the one only Rachel knew, and it had served to push him away. Not in the way she'd feared, maybe. Not because he considered her impossibly soiled and beyond redemption, because he'd sworn she wasn't. But because he might refuse in the future to contribute to her shame.

She didn't believe he understood what she'd tried to tell him—that it had been different with him. She wasn't sure she understood it herself, why that should be. She suspected it might have something to do with the fact that she trusted Sean Hussey. Right down to her soul, she did.

She'd trusted Ben too, in a way. Not the same way. Ben had been a maverick. Though he'd never set out to hurt her, he was capable of most anything. Like many of the men she brought up to this room, he'd wanted only to pound into her.

Not like Sean. Sean had touched her. He'd touched her gently and lit her up in a way she'd never seen coming.

Now he would never touch her that way again. He'd say such relations were beneath her. That she was worth more than lying with him.

When all she wanted was that feeling over again. The freedom of it, as if his touch had burned away all the chains that had weighed on her. As if for the first time she'd been a real woman.

She pulled her face from the damp pillow and rolled onto her back in the bed. Slowly and carefully, she touched her own naked body. Sean had touched her here. Her breasts. He'd suckled from her, starting a right swell of sensation. He'd run his palm down her belly and between her thighs. Invaded her with his fingers before anything else.

By the time they'd rocked together, she wanted him so much it was as if her whole body reached for him.

She'd been present, both that time and again when they'd sort of gravitated together during the night. Holding, holding to one another.

Maybe she didn't have to despise her body. Because for the first time in a long while, it had been hers. And, owning it, she had given it joyfully to him.

A wonderful gift even if it never happened again.

She had to get hold of herself. Climb from the bed, get dressed. Embark on her day. Go see Luke. Should she tell Rachel what had happened?

No, this was her secret. Hers alone.

****

To say Sean felt disconcerted would be an

understatement. He fetched up out on the street in front of the saloon with his mind in a fog, unable to think of much besides—

Sarah.

A storm of conflicting emotions possessed his heart. Grief and anger and indignation on her behalf, the fierce desire to make it right somehow for this woman who, deep inside, was still the little girl who'd stood on the platform with him. She'd had no one to stand up for her in a long while. Not, certainly, since she'd arrived here in Clabber Mills. Probably not before, either, on the streets of New York. They'd all looked after themselves then.

He didn't know how she'd endured what she had. He'd had no idea that was going on when he'd left here ten years ago. Would it have made a difference? He'd been trying to save himself then.

If he'd known, he'd damn sure have tried to help her.

Because she was Sarah. The quiet girl who, even on the trip out from New York, had carried a certain sweetness in her clear blue eyes. A sweetness that, beneath the pain, endured yet.

Who would have thought that such a girl-turned-woman, so contained and quiet, could have fired up the way she had in his arms last night? He'd never felt the like. As soon as she'd started kissing him, the heat had risen. When she'd shed her clothes… And, God, when he'd put his mouth to her breast…

Damn it, he wanted it all over again. But how could he ever approach her without her thinking he had used her, even as that bastard Gregson had? He'd paid for her last night, God damn it.

The very thought made him flush with shame and

remorse. What must she have thought? Sarah—lovely Sarah.

Maybe he could make up for it now. For she was no longer on her own. He was here for her. He had the means to help.

He stood surveying the street, and his eyes lit on the bank down the way. As soon as it opened, he'd go in and set her up with an account. Wire the funds in from out west where he had his stash. Then maybe hunt around for a property he could buy so she and her boy could move in. Get her out of the hell hole at his back, where she got struck in the face and had to accept, in her bed, random farmhands with the price to pay.

He'd set all that up and go back and tell her tonight. Maybe they could—

No.

Damn it, how was he going get the woman out of his blood?

He'd come back here to pay Bennie Clabber what he deserved. To see Jenny and maybe tell her what she meant to him. Not for Sarah.

But how could he turn his back on her now?

He went to the diner for some breakfast. By the time he finished, the bank had opened and he took care of business there. Matters were complicated by the fact that he didn't know Sarah's married name, so he set up the account in his own name, figuring he could transfer it to her later.

Then he went in search of property.

The land agent, an anemic-looking, middle-aged man called Scaggs, warmed to Sean when it emerged he was fully funded to buy. He trotted out all kinds of properties. Half the landowners in the county, so it seemed, were looking to sell. Others might be persuaded. Times were hard, which explained why Mr. Scaggs leaped on him quite so eagerly.

There were a few houses in town and more on failed farms outlying. Since he didn't think Sarah would be prepared to run a spread, he hesitated over those. Her boy would have to get to school. But once he deeded the property to her, Sarah could always rent out the land for extra income.

It delighted him that she—a rat from the streets of New York just like him—might become a property owner in her own right.

They made a list of properties for him to view. On impulse, he said to Scaggs, "What about the Clabber farm? Bennie Clabber's. That for sale?"

Mr. Scaggs sat forward in his seat, his pale eyes fixed on Sean's face. "Why? What have you heard?"

Sean had heard nothing. The query had come from nowhere. But he quickly zeroed in on Scaggs' question. "A few whispers here and there."

Scaggs lowered his voice. "It's true Clabber's farm is in heavy debt. These past few years when the crops failed—it took a toll. Then there was Mrs. Clabber's illness."

"She's been sick?"

"You know the Clabbers?"

"Used to."

"Mrs. Clabber had a stroke."

"Shame." It was a shame the cold stick of an old woman had survived.

"Indeed, indeed."

"The farm for sale?" Sean asked, a new form of revenge taking root in his mind.

"Not by the Clabbers, no." Mr. Scaggs hesitated. "Mr. Bennet Clabber borrowed from his brother at the mill till the senior Mr. Clabber could lend him no more. Then, he was forced to borrow elsewhere. His debtors might be willing to sell that debt."

"You don't say?"

"I do, though you didn't hear it from me."

"It's a good farm. How would I get in touch with these lenders?"

"You'd have to travel to Indianapolis. The Maxwell brothers. You heard of them?"

Sean shook his head.

"They're in the business of money, so to speak. Of loans to distressed property owners. No idea if they're near to foreclosing on Clabber."

Sean thought on that. He'd come back to kill Bennie Clabber. Nothing saying he couldn't watch him lose his farm first. The same farm where he, Sean, had been enslaved.

"Mr. Scaggs, I'd be right grateful for the Maxwells' direction."

Chapter Sixteen

"Sean, where were you? I was ever so concerned. And Cyrus was furious you didn't come home last night."

Sean performed a swift assessment of Jenny, who stood in front of him. She'd pulled her chestnut-colored hair up into a bun, but the pretty curls were escaping in the morning heat. She had her fingers twisted in her apron, and worry flickered in her eyes.

"Didn't take it out on you, did he?" Sean saw no new bruises. The old ones were fading to yellow and green. He still didn't understand how a man could hit a woman. His pa never had. He'd adored Ma just like Sean had. Losing her on the trip from Ireland had sent him on the downward spiral that had brought Sean—well, here.

Jenny shook her head. Another curl escaped.

Gently he told her, "Didn't I say I was here to conduct some business? That means I might have to see people from time to time."

"But—at night?" Her gaze was troubled. "Cyrus was real clear about the curfew."

"Curfew," Sean muttered. He hadn't had one of those settled on him since he'd left Clabber's farm. "Does he need me to leave?"

"He'll talk to you tonight." She hesitated. "Maybe at the end of the week."

Tight bastard wouldn't give up a penny of that

dollar, however reluctant he was to keep Sean here.

"Would you like some breakfast? We ate before Cyrus left, but I could make you something."

"I ate at the diner. Had some things to settle at the bank."

"Lunch then, in a while. I'm just scrubbing the stove."

He looked at her again. Last he'd been in the kitchen, he could have seen his face in that stove.

"Jenny, the house is clean. And he ain't here standing over you."

She began to cry. "It's just—oh, I shouldn't say." Her wide brown eyes met his and flitted away. "Shouldn't say to you."

"Jenny, go make us a cup of tea. We'll sit and talk, right?"

He followed her into the kitchen which, to him, looked immaculate. She removed the pot of blacking from the stove and stared at it helplessly.

"I'm stupid, Sean. I don't have a fire going. Lemonade?"

"That would suit me even better. And don't call yourself stupid."

"It was what Mrs. Riles always called me. Stupid girl. I started believing it."

She bustled around, poured the lemonade, and put out a plate of her shortbread.

"And she was right."

"She wasn't."

"I do stupid things all the time, which just makes Cyrus angry with me."

"I think it's more a case of Cyrus having a permanent angry on. He takes it out on you because he can. Sit down, honey, and tell me what's bothering you."

"I can't." But she sat across from him.

"I'm your friend, ain't I? Friends confide in one another."

"But…" Her cheeks flamed pink. "I've never talked about—well, women's things. With a man."

Lord have mercy. Maybe he didn't want to hear this.

"It's just that," her gaze dodged away from his again, "I got my monthly this morning. My women's monthly. That means—"

"I know what it means."

"I was so disappointed. Every month I hope— I'll have to tell Cyrus later. I thought if the house was real clean when he got home, well at least he couldn't find fault with that."

"Jenny. Jenny, look at me. You can't live like this, honey, afraid all the time. Worried you'll upset that—upset Cyrus. He's a small man, Jenny. Any fellow who takes out his temper on his woman is a small man."

"He's my husband."

"No matter."

"Besides, what else am I supposed to do? If I left him, where could I go?"

"I told you, I'll help. You could leave Clabber Mills. You sure you don't have any relations anywhere?"

She shook her head.

"Jenny, there's a whole big world out there. I've seen plenty of it. You don't have to live in purgatory here." He sat back in his chair. "If you could choose to do anything, anything at all, what would it be?"

"I hardly know. I haven't thought."

"Think about it for a minute. You have a dream? I'll help you reach it."

"A dream?" She sounded like she didn't understand the concept. Then, "You'd help me how?"

"I've got some funds put aside," he told her just as he had Sarah. "I can finance what you want to do."

"Funds?" Her gaze grew still wider. "You must be a man of means."

"I've done all right." He'd come west on the train with but one skill, and that was thieving. Bennie had taught him other skills on the farm. Funny how being a thief, turned respectable, had got him where he was.

If he could, in truth, be called respectable.

"By God," Jenny said with something like awe, "you and Rosalee are the only ones out of us who did all right. I suppose Milo will do well for himself once he marries Temperance and inherits the farm. But I reckon he'll have a long wait, because Mr. Bligh still looks hale and hearty. Oh, Sean, I fear for Milo. I do think he's making a mistake. And I understand what it is to make a mistake in marriage."

Sean feared for Milo too. He would be enduring his purgatory ahead of his reward.

"And Sarah. Poor Sarah." Tears flooded Jenny's eyes. "It's worse for a woman. A woman has to be careful. She steps out of line, this town can turn on her real quick."

She mopped her cheeks, for the tears had started to fall. "Oh, why couldn't I just have a child and—and fit into the life I was meant to have?"

"I'm telling you, Jenny, you can get away from this town before it has a chance to turn on you. You're young yet. You don't have to stay here and endure what Cyrus dishes out."

"Sean, I'm not strong enough."

"Then get strong. Honey, you're not that little girl standing on the station platform anymore."

"I wish you were right."

"I am. Give what I've said some thought."

"Dreams," she said almost wistfully.

"Dreams. And when Cyrus gets home tonight, I'll be here to talk to him."

****

Cyrus came in hot, primed for a fight. Sean made sure he was in the parlor where the man could see him right off, thinking to distract him from Jenny, who bustled between the kitchen and the dining room, setting up supper.

Cyrus stomped in, shedding sawdust all over Jenny's clean floor, and stood glowering at Sean from the parlor doorway. Sean took his time glancing up from the papers he studied.

"I want a word with you, Mr. Hussey."

"Do you?"

"Where the hell were you last night? Didn't I make it clear you had to be in by ten? It's damn inconsiderate for you to expect my wife to get up from our bed and let you in any later'n that."

"You're right, that would be inconsiderate. But I didn't require her to get up from your bed, did I?"

"We didn't know you weren't intending to show up. Anyway, this is a respectable household that caters to a respectable class of boarder, not the sort who stays out carousing all night long."

Sean felt like saying respectable men didn't hit their wives. He refrained.

"Anyway, I heard tell you were in the saloon last night." Cyrus barreled on. "In fact, I heard you stayed there all night. With that trollop Sarah Rupert."

Jenny, who listened from the dining room, suddenly went still. Sean fought down a swell of dismay. What would she think of him now?

Slowly he got to his feet. "Not that it's any of your business, but there was a little altercation at the saloon last night. I stayed to make sure Mrs. Rupert was all right."

"Oh, I'll just bet you did." Cyrus scowled. "Anyway, what's a—altercation?"

"A fracas. Sarah got hit in the face."

Jenny gasped, but Cyrus didn't give her a chance to speak.

"The woman's a whore and deserves what she gets if she's smacked."

"Just like your wife deserves what she gets?" Sean would have caught back the words if only for Jenny's sake. Too late.

"My wife's a respectable woman. And it's my duty to correct her when she needs it."

"Correct her?" Like a dog or a horse.

"When it's called for, yes. I'll thank you not to compare her to the likes of Sarah Rupert."

Sarah. Her soft lips parting beneath his own. Her breasts silken beneath his palms. The way she'd trembled just before he'd entered her.

"And I'll thank you to speak of Mrs. Rupert a bit more respectfully."

"Why? She your lover now?" A scornful smile stretched Cyrus's lips. "I've heard of men going soft over the whores they bed. Damn fools."

Somehow, Sean kept from knocking that smile off Cyrus's face. "Yeah, because only a fool would go soft over a woman, right?"

"Damn right. God made us *men*."

Sean wanted to walk out then. He wanted to let Cyrus keep the rest of his dollar and find lodgings elsewhere. Anywhere. But if he surrendered his place here, how would he keep an eye on Jenny?

She was going to need his support. Right up to the minute he convinced her to leave this sack of shit. For him? That remained to be seen.

Chapter Seventeen

When Sarah came downstairs the next morning, Stu gave her a share of the dollar Sean had paid him and eyed her closely. "You all right, Sarah? Your face looks pretty sore."

"It's not too bad."

She wanted to refuse the money, since it had been Sean, and she hadn't taken him to her bed for the money. That had been something else, something so far beyond anything she'd ever experienced at the hands of a man, she had no name for it. Except, *making love*. Maybe they had been making love.

But she needed the money. School would start soon and she'd be darned if her boy turned up there looking a disgrace. Bad enough the children called her what they did. He would have new britches. And shoes that fit.

She would go and pick him up from Rachel's today. Take him to the general store. Only—

There'd been plenty of people in the bar last night and the trouble had drawn everybody's attention. It would be all over town this morning. People would know where she'd got the money to outfit her son.

For a moment despair touched her heart. Luke deserved better than this. As for her—well, she no longer knew what she deserved.

Stu asked, "You think he'll come back tonight, that fellow you took upstairs?"

She hoped so. If she still believed in prayers, she would pray so.

"'Cause I have no doubt that Donny Ransom will be back. He wants what he wants."

"Donny Ransom?"

"That farmhand who was so set on taking you upstairs. He's not the sort to accept a no."

She couldn't. She really couldn't, not after being with Sean.

"Don't know," she told Stu. "I guess I'll worry about it when it happens."

She went out into the daylight. It was barely nine o'clock and already so hot you could fry eggs on the street. She remembered days like this on Gregson's farm, weeding row after row of corn or walking behind the plow horses, planting. There'd been days she thought she would die.

There'd been nights she wanted to.

She walked down to Rachel's place. Rachel was elbows-deep in her laundry tub out in the yard and looked up at Sarah when she entered the gate. At least, Sarah thought, the clothes would dry quick when Rachel got them on the line.

Sarah managed a smile. Should she confide in Rachel about what had happened last night or continue holding it to her heart?

Rachel got to her feet. "Sarah? What happened to your face, honey?" She hurried to where Sarah stood and touched the shiner gingerly with her wet, soapy hand.

"Had some trouble at the saloon last night. I got in the way."

"Oh, Sarah!" The distress in Rachel's eyes exceeded Sarah's own. "I tell you, you've got to stop working at that place."

"And do what? You know I'm fit for nothing else."

"You're not fit for getting knocked around, either. Sarah, honey, I beg you to look for work somewhere, anywhere else. If you don't get out of there it's going to end bad for you."

"I tried looking for work after Ben died. You know I did. It would be twice as hard now. Who'd hire a woman who—"

She broke off as both boys came out into the yard. Luke's curly head was the exact color of Ben's—dark brown. He looked more and more like his father as he grew, though he had her blue eyes.

They flew to her face and widened.

"Hello, boys." Sarah summoned up another smile that felt strained. "Luke, I've come to take you to buy your things for school."

His gaze questioned her but he said nothing.

"Come along now."

"Danny, you'll stay here and help me."

"Aww, Ma! That's women's work."

"It's work that keeps us clean is what, and it ain't beneath you."

At least Rachel was raising her son right.

Sarah took Luke's hand and turned back for town. Not till the little house was out of sight did Luke ask in a whisper, "Ma, what happened to your face?"

"Oh, just a little trouble at work last night. Wasn't meant for me."

"Does it hurt?"

"Not very much."

Luke contemplated that for a moment before he burst, "I can't wait to grow up."

"Can't you, son?"

"Then I can get me a gun and I'll shoot anybody that hurts you. Or who talks about you, either."

Sarah's blood went cold. This was not the ambition a mother wanted to hear from her son.

"Luke, honey, I'm touched you'd want to stick up for me. But people in our world can't just go around shooting other people. It's not the answer."

"Well, I'm sick of it," he said, sounding so much like Ben it startled her all over again. "At least if I had a gun, they might be more careful about what they say."

"Luke." She turned and faced him there in the dusty road with the sun beating on her head. "You might hear some people talking in town today. About me. About what happened at work last night. I want you to just let that talk go, understand?"

He gave her a glare that held both outrage and disquiet. "It ain't fair."

Tears stung the backs of Sarah's eyes. How many times had she gasped or sobbed those same words to herself? After Thaddeus Gregson had left her in her sleeping place, torn and aching. When she felt the constraints of the ties that bound her. And after Ben had died.

Somehow it seemed even more painful hearing her boy say them. Bad enough she'd been trapped in a life she didn't want. She'd hoped better for him.

"Listen to me, Luke. Plenty of things don't seem fair when they happen. Those things help us grow stronger. Now come along. Let's get what you need for school."

She stretched her share of Sean's money as far as she could, bought Luke a pair of shoes just a little too big for him, so they might still fit later. The jacket and trousers he so desperately needed. She'd hoped there'd be enough to treat him to lunch at the diner, but there wasn't. And that was all right because—

People did stare. Not just the women they encountered, but the men. They talked behind her back and behind their hands. Enduring more of that at the diner would be a trial.

On their way back to Rachel's, she saw a man approaching on horseback. When he drew near enough and hauled on the reins, she realized it was Sean.

Her reaction to seeing him shocked her—quick and visceral, mixed with an awkwardness caused by having Luke at her side.

Sean quickly dismounted and tipped his hat at her. "Sarah." He focused on Luke. "This must be your boy."

"Yes. Luke, this is Mr. Sean Hussey. He was off the orphan train back at the same time I was."

Luke eyed the man before him with interest, his gaze moving from the fine hat to the clear gray eyes before fastening on the sidearm. "You were an orphan train boy?"

"Yes, Luke, I was."

"But I thought orphan train kids never amounted to much."

"Luke!" Sarah exclaimed, but Sean just laughed.

"Some of us do." He switched that clear-eyed gaze to Sarah. "You working later?"

Her pulse leaped. "Yes."

"Oh. I thought you might take the night off, due to—" He gestured at her face.

"I'll be there."

"I'll stop by."

Her pulse leaped still more wildly. Was he saying

what she thought, what she hoped? Was there any chance he wanted to be with her again even half as much as she wanted to be with him?

But he said, "I've got something I'd like to talk over with you."

She fought to discipline her disappointment. "All right."

Sean turned back to Luke. "It was a pleasure meeting you, young man." He put out his hand and, after a moment's hesitation, Luke shook it.

"Sarah, I'll see you later."

It was a hope and a promise Sarah held to herself all the way to Rachel's and back to the saloon again.

Chapter Eighteen

Everyone in the saloon watched them, that evening. If there were more men crowded in than usual, it was probably because they'd come to stare. Maybe hoping Donny Ransom would also show up and they'd catch a brawl.

But Donny didn't show up. Maybe he couldn't get free from his farm duties. Maybe he'd been suitably intimidated by Sean so that contrary to what Stu had suggested, he wouldn't try again for Sarah's company. Her relief was surpassed only by her gladness that Sean arrived early.

Come to see her and nobody else.

She didn't want to admit that she'd fussed with her appearance this evening. She knew she wasn't pretty. And the reddened, purple patch on her cheekbone didn't help any. But she'd taken time over her hair and donned her favorite dress, striving hard not to look like a whore.

She didn't want Sean to think of her that way. On the other hand, she wanted very much for him to go upstairs with her again. What did that make of her?

They sat at the same table as last time, almost as if it was their table, and Sarah tried to ignore the stares. She ordered two whiskeys and left hers standing in front of her.

"That's a fine boy you have there, Sarah," Sean began, which lit her up with pride.

"He's a good lad at heart, though he struggles a bit with not having a pa, and with…what folks say about me."

Sean shot a look around the room and the patrons quickly glanced away. He'd handled himself well last night. Sarah didn't think anyone would take him on.

"Sarah…" He brought his gaze back to her. "I have some ideas I'd like to run past you. Now, I want you to know I'm not forcing anything on you. These are just suggestions. I'd like to help."

"Help?"

"Get you out of here. Away—away from this."

Sarah's breath stopped in her throat. What was he saying? That he considered taking her on—her and Luke? Marrying her? She must be asleep and dreaming.

"Help," she repeated. "How?"

"I've been talking with Mr. Scaggs at the land office and spent part of today viewing some properties. I'd like to take you tomorrow to look at a couple of them. If you're agreeable and you like what you see, I could set you up there. Get you out of—well, what you're doing now."

"Set me up?" She searched his eyes. "What exactly does that mean?"

"Oh, not what you're thinking." He grimaced. "Not what that sounded like, I guess. I wouldn't expect—expect anything in return. Since it would be my property free and clear, you could stay there without rent and I could maybe make you an allowance till you find out what sort of work you want to do, and get on your own two feet."

"Why? Why would you do such a thing as that?"

"I don't like seeing you here, Sarah. And I don't

think you've had a fair shake. If you'd accept a helping hand—"

Sarah's thoughts raced, as did her emotions from shame to hope to chagrin. She could escape this. Give Luke a better life. But—

"Wouldn't I just be beholden to you then, Sean?" Was that what she wanted?

He shrugged. "You wouldn't be beholden to me. No strings attached, like I say. Just a friend helping a friend who needs it."

Sarah didn't see how she'd fail to owe him for putting a roof over her head. But she didn't say so. "You can afford to do that? Just buy up a property?" What had he been doing out west?

"I can. Lots of properties going below their value here right now. The way I see it, buying property is never a bad investment."

Not an offer of marriage then, or any equivalent. Just a business deal. And a kindness. An act of wondrous generosity.

What should she do? The life she now lived might well be all she deserved, but she wanted better for Luke. Much better. A hand up, like Sean said, rather than a handout.

He sat and sipped his whiskey and watched while she struggled through the thoughts in her head. After a few minutes he said, "Sarah, I hope you won't let your pride get in the way—"

"Pride?" She stared at him. "You think I have any of that left?"

"I think you should."

"How? People are staring at me. Calling me *whore* in their heads and sometimes out loud. Wondering if you're going to go upstairs with me again."

Their eyes met for a long moment.

Sean drew a breath. "I told you, there are no strings attached to this. I wouldn't expect anything in return. What happened last night—" He stopped abruptly.

Sarah waited to hear what he had to say.

"I didn't expect that to happen, either," he concluded.

"You were protecting me."

"I'm sorry, Sarah, if you think I took advantage. That wasn't my intention. I'd be even sorrier if I thought what happened between us might put you off accepting help from me. It shouldn't. The five of us who got off the train here so long ago are the only thing I've got left of family. Rosalee—well, it seems she's doing all right. Milo has chosen his path. The way I see it, you and Jenny could use my help."

Her and Jenny. He had no special feelings for her, then, despite what had taken place between them last night. The tenderness. And the passion.

Suddenly she wanted to weep, her emotions threatening to overwhelm her. Disappointment and despair. This was what happened when a woman let her guard down, let her emotions out of the box where she'd kept them shut away so long. They betrayed her.

But for all that, she couldn't regret what they'd done last night. No.

"Sarah." He reached across the table and touched her hand. "Let me help you."

"That's what you want, is it?"

"Yes."

She lifted her gaze to him again. "Like—like a sister?"

He hesitated. Some emotion flickered in his pale gray eyes. "Maybe not quite like that."

"You figuring on doing something similar for Jenny?"

"Not sure what I can do for Jenny. Cyrus has her pinned down tight. Anything I try to do might come back on her. I need to give some thought to that. Meanwhile," he leaned across the table, "I can get you out of here. Make your life better."

A smile—or maybe it was a grimace—twisted her lips. "And what do you think people will say if you go buying a house and setting me up in it? You know very well what they'll say."

"They'll be wrong, won't they?"

Would they? The idea of living in Sean's house, maybe welcoming him there of the nights, made her ache she wanted it so much. And that meant it was a bad idea. She'd learned most everything she wanted was a bad idea.

So she shook her head. "I don't want to owe anyone. I'll look after my son, my way."

He kindled. "You'd rather have to go upstairs with the likes of that joker from last night? As I've said, you wouldn't owe me anything."

"And I've said, I don't take men upstairs often. I needed to buy Luke some school things—"

He dug in his pocket, brought out a handful of money and laid it on the table in front of her.

"There. Now you won't have to do that anymore, least for a time."

Stu appeared almost magically with a second whiskey for Sean, which he slid onto the table. Even as Sarah stared, appalled, he lifted an eyebrow at Sean.

"Mister, you stayin' the night again?" Deftly he extracted a dollar from the pile and walked away.

Dead silence met his departure. Sarah could no longer look at Sean, and shame stained her cheeks. The murmurs of other conversations went on around them and the rest of the money lay untouched on the table.

"I'm sorry," Sarah said at last. "He shouldn't have done that. Since you've already paid, you're welcome—welcome to stay. If you don't want to—"

"I didn't say that."

Hope and despair warred once more in Sarah's heart. Why did it have to be this way? She wanted him. But she didn't want him like this.

"Sarah, honey, I don't want me helping you to rest on anything we might do upstairs. Because it doesn't rest on that, understand?"

She nodded and lifted her gaze once more to his. "Stay," she whispered. "Stay the night."

Chapter Nineteen

This time, Sean had only two whiskeys under his belt when they went upstairs. He wasn't anywhere close to what he could call drunk, and even as he climbed the wooden stairs with Sarah, he knew it probably wasn't a good idea.

He'd been a boy and had grown into a man who disciplined his impulses. If he hadn't, he probably wouldn't have survived. It had taken nearly five years and a considerable amount of growth on poor rations for him to strike back at Bennie Clabber. And when he had, nothing good had come of it.

Or had it? The beating Bennie gave him in retaliation had pushed him to light out of Clabber Mills. And that in turn had started him on a life of risk, crime, and profit.

He turned and looked at the woman who had led him into the dusky room. He could still hear voices from downstairs, and he wondered if they were talking about him coming back up with her again.

He didn't worry about that so much as about Sarah herself.

She was not the woman he'd assumed she was when first he came back to Clabber Mills. He found her far deeper and far more complicated than that. While he'd been away, his focus had all been on Jenny. Sweet Jenny who'd always drawn his eye and his sympathy.

For Sarah, yes, he'd felt a sort of kinship. That of two children set adrift in the same hell. He was appalled by the life she lived now, and he'd do anything he could to help her out of it.

So what was he doing standing here contemplating removing his clothes, and hers, once more?

He wanted to. He wanted her, he couldn't say he didn't. Ever since last night he'd been able to think of little else. Even while he'd made plans to try and help her, it had been there, constant, in the back of his mind...

The way she'd trembled in his arms when he'd plunged into her. The way she'd clung to him as they rocked together. The intensity and the heat.

Who'd have thought it of quiet little Sarah?

"Sarah, honey," he began, feeling his way. "We don't have to do anything—"

"No?"

"No. Not anything you don't want."

She swallowed. He heard her distinctly in the quiet room. She lifted her chin. "What if I do want, Sean? What does that make of me?"

In two steps he had her in his arms. And it was as if a hard fist that had clutched at his guts all day long suddenly let go of him. This—this was what he'd been craving. And her too, by the feel of it. She came right up on her tiptoes and wound her arms around his neck. They kissed.

But no, that wasn't the word for it. Too wild to be a mere kiss, too demanding. They consumed one another there in the half dark and from the instant their lips met, there could be no question how this would end.

He knew that, even as they stumbled to the bed. As she lay there on the rough sheets, quivering beneath him, and him so desperate with need all his thoughts burned away. As joined above and below, he breathed her name into her.

Sarah. *Sarah.*

After, he still couldn't think. He lay breathing, just breathing, feeling her lying warm against him. Trying to gather the remnants of his sanity, which had flown away when he shattered.

This could not be good. He'd returned here to Clabber Mills in order to settle Bennie. And to find Jenny. Tell her—tell her what she'd always meant to him.

And here he lay in another woman's arms. Not just another woman. Sarah. How had that happened?

He lay trying to figure it, trying to keep breathing. Sarah ran her lips across his cheek to the corner of his mouth. She sucked on his lips one after the other.

He felt the tension gather inside him again, felt himself rise. By God, was that all it took from this woman? He'd never, so he swore on his life, known the like.

But he still craved the taste of her. The feel of her. He liked the way her heartbeat accelerated wildly beneath his lips when he put them to her breast. He liked the scent of her which now surrounded him here in her bed.

He liked that he could feel her mind moving, and her spirit. Quiet Sarah, who'd been through so much yet could still reach for him.

"Sarah, honey."

"Um?" She leaned up and put her tongue between his lips. She didn't say much. She was quiet even when they rocked together. But he sensed that she felt her way toward something as foreign to her as it was to him.

"Sarah, you keep doing that and I'm going to get all heated up for you again."

She slid her hand down his body from his chest to his stomach and lower, to wrap her fingers around him.

"Go ahead. Get all heated up."

"It's my understanding that women, well, women take a while to get receptive again."

"It's my experience that men do. Seems, Sean Hussey, you defy logic."

There was, so Sean decided, a burning pit of desire that just opened up, kind of like a blazing furnace, when Sarah touched him. He tended to fall right in.

"Sarah, honey," he said again, struggling against the flames and the motion of her fingers, "I don't want you to think—"

"I don't want you to think, either, Sean. I've never felt this way for anyone. Never."

Were those tears he heard in her voice? No time to tell, because she ran her lips down his body, following the path of her fingers, and he went straight to heaven.

****

Sarah slept. She awoke again. Even in sleep, she remained aware of Sean there beside her. The taste of him stayed in her mouth and the warmth of him surrounded her. A rare comfort.

When awake, she lay and tried to figure out what made being with this man so different. What turned being claimed by him from horror into such sharp pleasure?

When Mr. Gregson had first come to her sleeping place back on the farm, she'd been an untouched girl, hurting and frightened, trying to get along in this new life where she'd landed. She'd been suffused with horror at what he'd done to her and terrified by the various threats that accompanied the repeated act.

You'll keep quiet about this, girl. Or you'll be sorry. You'll feel my strap on your nice little bum. I'll toss you right out of here and when winter comes you'll freeze to death. It's all you're good for anyway. Your mother was probably a whore. Wasn't she? Didn't want you. But so long as you can spread your legs, girl, you'll serve a purpose.

Spread your legs.

That last had been his favorite order to her and had drilled deep into her brain. After the fear she felt had come anger. She'd discovered, though, that anger brought worse pain. And so she'd learned to shut a door in her head when Mr. Gregson entered her tiny, airless room. She'd learned to slam it shut more and more quickly until only blackness came when he attacked her. She shut herself away from what was happening so completely it might have been happening to someone else.

It had been a little different with Ben. Before they married there'd been only some kissing, in which Mr. Gregson never indulged, and a little groping. That had helped to, well, acclimate her. After, Ben had expected what he expected. On many occasions, the door had come to her rescue with Ben, and she'd let it slam shut.

Where was that door now?

She lay with her cheek on Sean Hussey's chest and wondered about it. What made this different?

Was it because she trusted Sean? Well, she'd trusted Ben too, or had come to trust him, if not quite in the same way. Ben was a different sort of man entirely from Sean. He'd had a wild look in his eyes sometimes, and wild ideas in his head.

He'd never hurt her, no. Yet still she'd slammed that door against him, the same one she employed when she brought the occasional man up here.

Except for Sean. With Sean, her fingers didn't even reach for the edge of the door...

She snuggled closer to him and listened to his heartbeat. A woman could anchor herself to a man like Sean. Could anchor her heart.

She'd never had much for her own. No family behind her, just her ma, who'd done the best she could. Few possessions. No real home. She'd had Ben for a while. She had Luke.

She wanted Sean.

She lay and contemplated that truth. It felt as strange as the pleasure he gave her. Because she'd thrust all that away from her too—wanting things. No use wanting things you couldn't have.

But now she'd had Sean Hussey and she wanted him, wanted him in her life. He'd made it plain, though, that he meant to help her as a friend. He hadn't come back to Clabber Mills for her. He'd returned to settle old scores and maybe for Jenny.

Jenny.

Then what was this about? This pull she felt to him and the pleasure they made when they came together?

It better not be love. She'd never been in love and didn't intend to start now.

Please, don't let this be love.

Chapter Twenty

Sean hummed with satisfaction when he drew the hired wagon up in front of the Three Feathers and helped Sarah in. Not just physical satisfaction, though that certainly made a part of it.

They'd risen together, Sarah displaying an unexpected amount of modesty as they dressed. He'd left her to finish getting ready while he went and hired the rig, and she came out to meet him looking—well, respectable.

As she was, he reminded himself. A widow doing what she must to provide for her son. She'd done her best to get Luke out of the atmosphere in which she had to work.

Now he'd get the both of them out.

She'd donned a plain dark blue dress and a little hat, and pinned her light brown hair up under it. The bruise on her cheek had started to fade. In the morning light Sean could see she'd patted some powder on over it, but no other paint. Her lips looked soft, and naturally pink.

He thought about where on his body those lips had been just last night, and hastily pushed the memory away. He had to act like a sane man this morning.

"We have one stop to make before we ride out to view the properties," he told her.

She looked inquiring. "Do we?"

"Yeah."

When he drew up outside the bank just a short way down Main Street, she looked surprised.

"Come in with me."

"Here?"

"Got some business to complete."

The bank manager, Mr. Beesom, took care of Sean personally, as he had the other day. When Sean announced he wanted to transfer the new account he'd opened into Sarah Rupert's name, Mr. Beesom looked questioning, and Sarah began to sputter.

"What? What are you—"

"It's just a safety net, Sarah. Something for you to fall back on. You and Luke."

She went silent with either shock or dismay. Sean couldn't really imagine what she was feeling. But when Mr. Beesom passed over the paperwork for her to sign and she saw the account balance, her eyes went round and her fingers trembled.

She didn't argue it in front of the rather intimidating bank manager. But when they got outside she turned to Sean in distress.

"Sean. It's too much."

"It isn't. Just enough to hold you till you figure out what you want to do and maybe help you get started on it."

"I've never had that much money before. I never really had any money, you know?"

"I know."

"What I did earn just flew from my fingers. Survival."

Sean chucked to the horse and they rolled out. "It feels strange at first, when you're used to having nothing. When Billie and I first started bringing in real money—

we were both off orphan trains, you see—we couldn't hardly believe it."

Sarah gazed away from him. "Maybe because we arrive with nothing and figure we'll die the same way. But Sean, how can I accept—" Her cheeks flushed violently. "I've done nothing to earn that. Have I?"

"No, honey. That account, it has nothing to do with—well, what you gave me last night." What could he do or say to settle her on that score? "I figure what you gave me was a gift."

She nodded, but she'd started to look miserable again.

He flicked the reins. "I've got three properties I'd like you to see today. I want you to try and look at them with an open mind as to what would be best for you and Luke. Try to picture yourselves living in each one. There's the matter of Luke getting to school. You don't want to be out too far. And you getting to town if you decide to take a job there. Also, there's how much you can look after comfortably.

"When I viewed them yesterday, I could see advantages and disadvantages to all three, and I want your opinion."

Sarah said nothing. They passed the Withers' little house, which stood quiet, the front garden neat as a pin, and Sean wondered what Jenny thought of the fact that he hadn't come back to his room again last night. What Cyrus had said. He'd probably toss Sean out on his ear.

Not till they'd passed the little house did Sarah say softly, "What's between you and Jenny, Sean?"

He pursed his lips. "Between us? She's a married woman. One whose husband abuses her."

"I know. He hits her."

"Not just that. He treats her like a dog. A dirty cur he doesn't like. Some people are right fond of their dogs. Not Withers."

"I see her in town sometimes, just in passing. We don't share more than a word or two. She always seems—"

"Worried?"

"Distressed, I'd say. Anxious to get away."

"He oversees her time. Oversees pretty much all she does. In his opinion, not much of what she does is good enough."

"That's awful. Sean, do you mean to help her too?"

He looked at her.

"The way you're helping me, I mean."

"If I can. It's a touchy situation, with Withers thinking he owns her."

"He does own her. Ben owned me, when we were married."

"You being a widow makes it easier. You can have your own property. Anything I give Jenny could fall into Cyrus's hands and it wouldn't do her a drop of good."

"So you've come back to act the part of a crusading angel?"

"No." Sean didn't want to lie to Sarah, not after all they'd shared. "I came back to give Bennie Clabber what he has coming. And that means whatever property I may decide to buy today will probably have to be put in your name. That way if I get arrested and put away—"

"Sean. No!"

"It could happen."

"Well, you can't let it happen. You've worked too hard to make something of yourself just to end up in prison. For murder."

"Sometimes killing's justified." He and Billie had always tried to keep from it. They might fire some shots, wing a guard or knock him over the head. But to his knowledge, they hadn't left anyone dead.

That could all change now. He wanted Bennie Clabber dead. And maybe Cyrus Withers. And, he thought judiciously, he might throw in Thaddeus Gregson for good measure.

If Cyrus did die, by some terrible accident perhaps, Jenny would become a widow. Just like Sarah.

Would he act on that?

He regarded Sarah out of the corner of his eye. What lay between them—the heat and the passion—had been completely unexpected. Did it change what he felt—what he'd always felt—for Jenny?

As of this moment he could not tell.

They turned up a dusty track toward a house that sat amid a garden every bit as well-tended as the Withers'. A story and a half with a small porch, the house was painted soft gray and looked neat as could be.

"Oh, Lord," Sarah whispered under her breath.

Sean shot her a look. "What is it?"

"This place—" she began, but a woman thundered out onto the porch. Large in girth, she squinted at them before an unhappy look overtook her face.

No sooner had Sean stopped the wagon in front of the steps than the woman cried, "What's she doing here? I thought Mr. Scaggs said a buyer wanted to view my property."

"He does." Sean disembarked and handed Sarah down like a fine lady. "Mrs. Walters? I'm the prospective buyer."

Mrs. Walters' face turned the color of an overripe

plum and her chin wobbled indignantly.

"Then why have you brought this—this woman?"

Sean's temper immediately rose, a fact he strove mightily to conceal.

Sarah tugged at his arm. "Sean, let's go."

"No. We've come to view the property and view it we will. Unless Mrs. Walters has decided she no longer wants to sell."

Mrs. Walters narrowed her eyes at him. "No, I want to sell. I plan to go live with my sister, since we're both widowed, and there's no sense keeping two households. I just don't understand why *she's* here. I know who she is and what she does for a living."

"Mrs. Rupert is also a widow, Mrs. Walters. She requires a place to live."

"I don't know about this. I thought Mr. Scaggs was sending me a respectable buyer. I wouldn't want to saddle my neighbors with such a one."

Sean glanced at Sarah. Tears had come to her eyes, and she clutched his arm for dear life. "If you prefer not to show us the property—"

Mrs. Walters sniffed. "I guess you can look. If you want."

They viewed the house and, after, the barn in near silence. Mrs. Walters contributed a word here and there explaining when something had been repaired or replaced. The interior of the house was as neat as the outside.

"Well?" Mrs. Walters demanded when they once more stood on the front porch.

"We'll take it under consideration and let Mr. Scaggs know our decision."

Mrs. Walters' sharp eyes moved between them.

"You getting married or something?"

Sean didn't answer but handed Sarah back up into the hired wagon like a queen. He'd had a taste, right enough, of her life. And he didn't like it one bit.

Chapter Twenty-One

As soon as the wagon rattled on down the track from Mrs. Walters', Sarah covered her face with her hands. She wished she could disappear right off the bench beside Sean.

Instead she said into her palms, "Well, that was humiliating."

"I'm sorry, honey."

Honey.

"She shouldn't have treated you that way. It wasn't right."

"As soon as I saw her and realized whose place that was, I knew she'd look down her nose at me. Her and that bunch of crones from the Women's Institute. Even when we came off the train, they looked at us like we were something scraped off a shoe."

"I don't remember her."

"You probably didn't run into her much. I did, when I went to town with Mrs. Gregson. And now—now it's even worse."

She took her face from her hands. "And that's a taste of what Luke gets when he attends school, isn't it? No wonder he's getting in fights all the time."

Sean said nothing. His profile had gone rigid and his pale eyes looked stark.

Grief filled Sarah as she went on, "I should have known better. Known better than to reach for anything respectable."

"Frankly, I don't think Mrs. Walters' house is good enough for you and Luke."

She gaped at him. "Not good enough? It's a little dream of a place."

He wrinkled his nostrils. "Had a stink, that place. Smelled sanctimonious."

That made Sarah hiccough a laugh. "Maybe so."

"We still have two other places to look at."

The second property was out on a lonely road hunkered down amid its fields, and it clearly needed some work. Sarah tried to look at it objectively. The elderly man showing it didn't know who she was, him being a relation of the out-of-town owner.

"I don't know," Sarah said when they left. "It's out pretty far for Luke to get to school. And only imagine this place in winter when the snows come." She could hardly believe they discussed a property—for her and her son.

"Fair enough. We have one left that we'll catch on the way back to town. I believe Mr. Scaggs said that one's empty right now. He's supposed to meet us there with the key."

The property was located on Irish Road. Sarah wondered if that was a good omen. As soon as they turned up the track, she exclaimed, "I know this place. Mrs. Hamilton and her sister used to live here. Mrs. Gregson would stop by when we were running errands."

"Mrs. Hamilton?"

Mr. Scaggs' horse stood near the front of the house, which had a sad air. The garden looked overgrown and wild. The roof sagged just a little. What appeared to be a washhouse and a shed stood to one side. The barn needed major repairs.

"Needs painting," Sean said as he helped Sarah down.

Mr. Scaggs came hurrying out to meet them and he too looked startled to see Sarah.

"Mr. Hussey. Mrs.—Rupert, isn't it?"

Sarah nodded. For some reason her throat had closed. Coming to this house had, in the past, been one of her few good memories. Mrs. Hamilton and her sister had always treated Sarah kindly. Offered her a cookie if she and Mrs. Gregson stepped in. Mrs. Hamilton had smiling blue eyes.

She and her sister had been among the few people who did not treat Sarah differently because she was a train girl.

And the scents here! The two elderly women had mixed herbal teas, one of which Mrs. Gregson purchased for a stomach complaint, and made herbal-scented soaps. It had always smelled wonderful.

Now Sarah stepped up onto the small porch where the two women used to sit in their rockers, long gone. The view from here would be of the gardens where the herbs grew and the dusty road beyond.

And when Sarah stepped in, following Mr. Scaggs, she thought she caught a faint whiff of those herbs as if they permeated the very wooden floor and walls of the place.

A parlor that seemed much smaller now that she was grown, with an equally tiny bedroom to one side. But the kitchen, built across the back of the building, opened up like a pair of welcoming arms, with a large cookstove and a wooden shelf stretching across the back wall, and plenty of space for another table where one might sit to have a cup of tea.

She stood there and drew in a deep breath, her senses clamoring. Peace lay here, or at least the possibility of it.

"Two more bedrooms upstairs," Mr. Scaggs said in a bored voice, apparently failing to perceive Sarah's emotional turmoil. "A work shed outside where the previous owner—"

"Sorted and dried herbs." Sarah said softly, and both men stared at her. "I remember that about Mrs. Hamilton and her sister."

"Well, then," said Sean, a bit puzzled. "Shall we view the upstairs bedrooms and go out to take a look?"

The bedrooms were indeed small, tucked under the eaves. Sarah didn't care. She already wanted this place with an unprecedented longing. The notion that she might live here, and the idea that such a wonder might be made possible by Sean, the man she—

Hastily she caught herself back. Don't go there. Don't even think such a thing.

She half listened while Mr. Scaggs outlined possible uses for the work shed. And the other, smaller building beyond. They peeked into the barn where daylight showed between the slatted boards. They turned and surveyed the house from the back.

Sarah said nothing, though she wanted to jump up and down with the rush of her emotions. Sean told Mr. Scaggs they would consider all three properties and let him know if any would suit. They walked out to the hired wagon and climbed inside.

Once they were rolling back toward town, Sean glanced at Sarah and asked, "Well what do you think, Sarah? That first property seems to be in the best condition, though, to be sure, the owner wasn't pleasant.

She don't matter, though."

When Sarah said nothing, he went on. "The second—"

"It seemed very lonely."

"Yes. A bit too far out for Luke to get to school. The third place," he shook his head, "that needs a lot of work."

"I want it," Sarah said clearly. She did not know when she'd last spoken those words, if ever. She'd thought them just recently when she'd ached for this man—this boy-turned-man—in her bed. Other than that, she did not believe she'd ever in her life reached for anything.

Sean gave her a sharp look. "You sure about that, honey? Like I say, it needs a lot doing to it. The downstairs is mostly all kitchen. Those bedrooms are pokey, and the garden's all gone wild. It needs painting inside and out. That's a lot to take on."

"I'm sure." She turned and looked at him, discovering to her dismay she had tears in her eyes.

Appearing startled now, Sean drew the wagon to the side of the road and took her in his arms where she wept all over the front of his fine coat.

They stayed like that with him just holding her till her tears died to hiccoughs and she drew far enough away to say, "I don't know what's the matter with me, honestly I don't."

Sean straightened her hat, which had gone askew. She had a sudden sensation of his fingers in her hair last night and just like that she could feel him, all of him.

"I'm usually able to keep my emotions under better control."

"Sarah, look at me."

She did. His cool gray eyes had warmed and turned kind.

"If you want that place, honey, it's yours."

She gasped.

"We'll go to Mr. Scaggs' office today and have him draw up the paperwork. I'll get you right out of that place where you're living. That is, if you don't mind things being rough for a time at your place."

Her place. A haven of her own, whatever she might make of it. She'd never dreamed of such riches.

But—what of everything else? Her job at the saloon, and bringing Luke out here where, yes, the house needed work. Maybe she could leave Luke with Rachel just a while.

She whispered, "How will l get to work?"

"Sarah." Sean touched her on the chin, urging her to meet his gaze again. "You don't have to work there anymore. You don't have to take men up to—well, upstairs with you. That's what the money at the bank is for. There's enough to set you on your feet until you figure out what you want to do."

"I know what I want to do. What Mrs. Hamilton did. Grow herbs and make soaps and teas—she used to call them tisanes. Restart her business. But it will take time."

"You've got your whole life, honey."

Sean chucked to the horse and they started away again.

Sarah's thoughts galloped ahead. If she no longer kept a room at the saloon, how would she see Sean? Would she ever have the pleasure of lying with him again? Would he ride out to see her at the tiny, herb-scented house?

Could she exist, if he didn't?

Chapter Twenty-Two

When Sean returned to the Withers' house late that afternoon, having concluded his business at the land office and returned the hired wagon to the livery, he found his belongings set out on the porch. He didn't have much other than what he customarily carried with him. Just the leather satchel and a few garments he'd left hanging in Jenny's spare room. But the message was clear.

He stopped where he stood on the porch steps wondering if there was any point trying to argue it. Cyrus would still be at work and Jenny likely had no say.

While he stood there pondering it, she came out onto the stoop. Her eyes were red from crying and she had a new bruise on her cheek.

"Oh, Jenny," Sean said. Was this his fault? Had his defiance of Cyrus's curfew made the man angry enough to hit her again? But why should he take out his anger with Sean on her?

"What happened?" He reached to touch her cheek and she drew away hastily before glancing around.

"No, Sean, somebody might see. Please take your bags and go."

Sean narrowed his eyes. "Why did he hit you?"

Her big, brown eyes swam with tears. "He was real angry that you didn't come home again last night. Called you all kinds of names. When I spoke up to defend you,

140

said something important must have come up with your business to keep you away, he got—well, suspicious. Asked me if I was fond of you. Told me I'd better never turn my eyes to any other man besides him, and well—"

"The bastard."

"I'm sorry, Sean. I've liked having you here, and having someone to talk with. But it was my fault—"

"It wasn't."

"I should have been more respectful. More careful what I said."

And why should a woman walk on eggshells in her own home?

"It's just the way he was talking about you. I know you're a good man."

For the second time that day, Sean reached out to take a weeping woman into his arms. Jenny, though, pulled away and backed through the door. "No! Someone will see us. Tell him."

"All right, honey. I'll go." He bent and gathered up his things. God knew where he'd stay tonight. His thoughts veered to Sarah and away again. He didn't want her feeling obliged to welcome him in return for the help he'd offered her.

"You need anything, Jenny, you come to me. Hear?"

He got madder and madder as he walked back to town. The rage burned up through him the way it used to do back when he had to take Bennie Clabber's orders. A combination of fury and resentment.

He was waiting, with his bag at his feet, when the day shift at the mill let out. The men who emerged, a sizeable crew, glanced at him curiously. Cyrus Withers came out in company with two of his cronies, laughing as if he hadn't left his wife in tears earlier that day.

Sean stepped up and punched Cyrus square in the face. He made the punch count and the smaller man staggered. His companions caught him so he didn't fall down. All three stared at Sean, who leaped forward and spoke into Cyrus's face.

"That's for your wife. In return for what you gave her." Just one punch, though he wanted to batter the man senseless. "From now on, anything and everything you do to her, I'll do to you in return."

"Why you—" Cyrus growled, and the blood started to stream from his nose. "What business of yours is what passes between me and my wife?"

"Never mind that. You just remember." Sean glanced at the other men, who all stared in shock. "D'you know he beats his wife? A little woman. He's a right big man, isn't he?"

The fellow on Cyrus's right bleated, "A man's got a right to hit his wife when she needs it."

"Oh, yeah?" Sean turned on the man. "And when does she need it, eh? When she's chased after your children all day and is so tired she burns your dinner? When among her hundred tasks she forgets one you deemed important? When she dares to have an opinion that's different from yours?"

The men departing the mill had formed a half circle. They now fell silent except for one man who exclaimed, "He's gone crazy."

Was it so crazy, Sean wondered, to allow women— and undervalued women, for that matter—their own feelings? To allow them to legitimize themselves by stating what they felt?

Before he could determine an answer, another man came stomping out from the mill. Of medium height, with light brown hair receding from his forehead, Sean had no trouble recognizing him as the mill owner, Conrad Clabber.

He wore a dusty blue suit and an outraged scowl on his face that made him look so much like his brother Bennie it sent a chill creeping up Sean's spine.

"What's going on here?" Clabber demanded. His gaze swept Cyrus, who still streamed with blood before moving to Sean. It narrowed. "I know you, don't I?"

Quite likely so. Conrad had seen Sean just recently at the cattle auction, and numerous times in his brother's company. But that had been years ago, and Sean had been no more than a boy. A nearly invisible boy.

"Sean Hussey," he introduced himself. "Your employee here, Cyrus Withers, has some accounting to do."

Clabber raised his eyebrows. "To you?"

"To the world at large. This man abuses his wife. Did you know that?"

Conrad stiffened. "None of my business. Or yours, I expect."

"I'd think you'd be ashamed to have such a sack of shit on your payroll."

Conrad sniffed, his little eyes turning colder. "Mister, if I fired every man who knocks his wife around from time to time, I'd have nobody on the payroll."

He swept the men surrounding them with a look. "Now, all of you clear out of here. Cyrus, you want me to send for the marshal?"

Cyrus dabbed at his bloody face again. "Nah. He didn't hurt me none." He drew away from his companions and spat at Sean, "You just watch out, Hussey. And keep your nose out of my personal business."

Sean stared him down coldly. The men moved off, leaving Sean and Conrad standing alone.

Conrad eyed Sean up and down once again. "I do know you, don't I? From some place."

"No." Sean turned on his heel. "But you will."

****

Since he wanted a drink after that, he headed for the Three Feathers. He wondered if Cyrus and his fellows would go there also, but when he went in he found the place nearly deserted. Too early for the serious drinkers, it seemed.

The barman, Stu, greeted him with raised eyebrows. "Whiskey?"

"Please."

"You lookin' for another night with Sarah? 'Cause she's upstairs. You can pay me if you like and I'll let her know."

Sean shook his head.

The barman drifted off, and Sean sat worrying about what he'd just done.

Had he been stupid, giving in to his impulses? Would Cyrus go home now and take his humiliation out on Jenny? Would he accuse her of things concerning him, Sean, that weren't true?

He'd learned long ago it wasn't wise to give in to impulses. Doing so often had bad consequences. But that had been when he was a boy who didn't own himself. He was a man now, who did.

Anyway, there were times when you just had to stand up and speak out. Follow those impulses even if it meant you paid a price after.

He had no idea where he would sleep tonight.

Impulse—impulse said he could ask Sarah to take him in for another night.

But. He didn't want her feeling obliged to do that in return for the help he was giving her, and if he thought he could share her bed and not make love to her, he was lying to himself.

Maybe he'd just sit here and drink all night. Just so long as he didn't get too drunk to draw his sidearm and aim straight, should Cyrus and his pals come looking for him.

Chapter Twenty-Three

When Sarah came down from her room at about eight o'clock that night, the first thing she saw was Sean sitting at the table in the corner. He had half a glass of whiskey set in front of him and rested his head on one hand, elbow propped on the scarred wood.

She hadn't meant to work tonight. In fact she'd come down to tell Stu so, if anyone asked for her. She wasn't dressed for the floor, still wearing the dress in which she'd gone out with Sean earlier and had spent the last hours packing, though she had precious little to gather up.

When she saw Sean, she crossed straight to his table, placed her hand on his shoulder, and leaned down. "Sean? Is something amiss?"

He looked up at her, his pale gray eyes—usually so cool—full of sorrow. Sarah caught her breath. Had something happened to prevent the sale of Mrs. Hamilton's house? Worse, was he regretting his generosity to her?

Oh, Lord, what would she do if she had to surrender that dream so newly hers? If she had to return to this life she lived?

He shook his head at her. A dull flush along his cheekbones argued the whiskey in front of him wasn't his first. "Sarah, I've done something stupid."

She slid into the chair beside his. "What have you

done?"

"I socked Cyrus Withers in the face."

"Cyrus—Jenny's husband?"

"Yeah. When I got back there today, she had new bruises on her face. So I waited for him outside the mill and paid him back."

"Oh."

He shot her a look. "You might say I'm here in Clabber Mills on a mission of payback. But now I'm thinking he's probably gone home and taken it out on Jenny. Sweet little Jenny. Getting battered because I couldn't keep hold of my temper."

Sarah's heart quivered in her breast. It sounded—it sounded almost as if Sean was in love with Jenny. And would that be so hard to believe? When Sarah was in love with him.

Sudden tears came to her eyes. "You jumped to her defense. Like a white knight." She, Sarah, wasn't the only one he had helped. Wanted to help. Yes, he'd spent a couple nights in her bed. Spent his passion on her. Only because she was available.

Jenny was not.

It hurt. It hurt like fire, because she knew better. She knew better than to open her heart. She should have kept that door tight shut, the one that had served her so well for so long. Instead, she'd gone and let Sean Hussey in.

Wrong. He'd always been there.

"Hell, Sarah, I ain't no white knight."

"You are. To me."

"If you only knew—the things I've done."

"We've all done things we're not proud of, Sean. God knows, I have. You think I'm proud of this life? It's called survival."

"I know. But what if he's gone home and battered her? What if he kills her? It can happen. Remember Nora Gray?"

Nora Gray had been a girl off another orphan train who had worked at a distant farm. It had got out eventually that her master had beaten her to death for spilling a churn of cream.

Thaddeus Gregson had made sure Sarah heard the story. "See what happens, girl, to a lass who gets stupid?"

In his case, stupid would be telling anyone what he did to her in the stifling dark of her little room. She'd got that message.

She shifted on her chair. "Do you want me to check on Jenny, Sean? I could walk down there in the morning, once Cyrus is gone to work. If I go now, he won't let me in."

Sean searched her face with those pale gray eyes. "Maybe a good idea. But meanwhile—"

"Meanwhile, I think you ought to stop drinking." She glanced down at the satchel under the table by Sean's feet. "Has Cyrus kicked you out? Do you have anywhere to stay tonight?"

He shook his head.

"Then you'll stay here with me."

"Sarah—I don't want you feeling you have to—"

"I don't feel any way, Sean." A pure lie. She fair ached to take him upstairs and make love to him. Real love. And that shocked her as much as anything. Because she'd spent so long disconnecting her feelings from the physical act that took place between a male and a female, it seemed like this was the first time.

He was her first. Her first lover. Her last.

Once again, tears came to her eyes. What was the

matter with her? She never let her emotions get out of hand like this.

"We don't have to do anything, Sean, if you don't want to. You lie on your side of the bed and I'll lie on mine." If he didn't want her, if he wanted Jenny instead, there was nothing she could do about it. She could bear it, couldn't she?

Maybe not.

He searched her eyes again. "The barman—"

"I'll take care of Stu."

She rose, went to the bar and leaned on it. "I'm takin' him upstairs, Stu."

"Good." The barman held out his hand.

"I'm not charging him."

"What?"

"I'm not doing it for the money, Stu. He's my guest."

"Listen here, Sarah. You work for the profit of this place, just like I do. Mr. Bracer won't like it."

"I don't care." She daren't share that she'd be leaving Mr. Bracer's employ soon. He might throw her out now.

Stu grunted. He did not look happy, but he jerked his head at the stairs.

Sarah led Sean up, carrying his bag for him. It wasn't very heavy, and she wondered what he had in there. They exchanged not so much as a word till they entered the room.

"You rest," she told him then. "Come morning, I'll go pay Jenny a visit, see how she's doing."

Sean sat on the side of the bed, since there really wasn't any other place to sit, and kicked off his boots.

Sarah wondered if he wished he were here with Jenny instead of her. Sweet Jenny, he'd called her, and that made Sarah's heart hurt. The most he wanted from her was friendship. Best she could do was be a friend to him. Support him if she could. Give him a place to put his head.

He lay back and stretched out on the bed, fully clothed except for his boots. "You know, Sarah, it ain't fair."

"What isn't?"

"The way women and kids get treated."

"Listen to you. Maybe you are a white knight after all."

"I mean it. When we were kids here, we got treated like dirt. Worse than dirt." He paused. "Jenny still is getting treated that way."

"Cyrus Withers is what Ben used to call a dumb-ass." She also hesitated. "Do you intend to do anything more about it?"

"What can I do?" Sean's eyes narrowed. "Well, yeah, I could kill him."

Then Jenny would be a widow. He could marry her. Sarah suffered a pang.

"Killing a man could bring you all kinds of trouble."

"Only if I get caught."

"Sean!"

"Something happens to him now, though—well everybody at the mill saw me take him on. I should have just laid in wait for him when he was on his way home. Then Jenny would be free of the bastard."

Sarah's heart fell violently. "Don't talk like that, now. Get some rest."

She took off her dress, only because she didn't want to wrinkle it, and lay down on the other side of the bed. The only light came in under the door, but she could hear

Sean breathing in the dark.

"In the morning, Sarah, you'll walk down and check on Jenny?"

Sarah squeezed her eyes shut against the pain. "I will."

So he lay there and worried about Jenny. Lay in her bed.

"Good. Good."

Sarah stared at the black ceiling until Sean's breaths grew deep and even. Then she wept.

Chapter Twenty-Four

Sean once more woke disoriented, not knowing where he was. The air in the room felt hot and close. A warm body lay next to him.

Sarah.

Everything fell into place then. He remembered it all. Getting thrown out of the Withers' house. Waiting for Cyrus at the mill. His worry for Jenny.

He'd been a fool. By now he should have learned how to hold onto his temper. Only—it hadn't been his temper this time so much as an inner demand for justice.

He folded his arm across his forehead and thought about it. The children who had come west on the orphan trains had no one to speak for them. No parents, most of them. No one to make certain they were all right. Sure, the Society had plucked them off the streets, given them clothing and a measure of sustenance, found people who agreed to take them in.

But once delivered to those people, the Society washed its hands of them. No one ever came back out to check whether the placements had been good ones. No one took the part of these children, or spoke up for them. They might as well be seeds cast adrift on the wind by an uncaring hand.

Sean had helped during enough planting seasons to know that not all seeds that were broadcast took root and thrived. The farmer did not come back and check on each and every one. Either they grew or they didn't. And like a returning orphan train, there was always another planting season.

He remembered standing on the station platform that hot summer's day with his four companions. They'd had no one to speak for them, other than him.

He hadn't done so then. Damned if he'd keep from doing so now.

He propped up on one elbow and looked at the woman who lay beside him. An unexpected rush of tenderness swamped him. She slept in her chemise, half turned toward him. Most of her hair had tumbled down during the night. She looked lovely, and so young.

Sarah was young, for all she'd endured. He tried to total it up in his mind. She couldn't have been more than ten or eleven when they'd arrived here, maybe less. Perhaps fifteen or sixteen when he'd left. She now had an eight-year-old son and couldn't be more than twenty-five.

He felt pretty confident he could help Sarah, get her started on a better life where she could maybe restore her reputation, though that wouldn't be easy. Not for her, or her son.

Jenny would be harder to help. Unless, yes, he killed Cyrus. And if he got caught, that could complicate things for the woman beside him.

He sat up on the side of the bed and the mattress tipped. Sarah stirred.

"Sean? It's early. Lie back down."

The building lay quiet and the square of the window remained dark gray. It must indeed be early.

"Sean—" She reached out and touched his arm. Tugged at him. Half against his will, he lay back down, and she moved into his arms.

She wore nothing but that thin chemise and the heat of her skin came right through it. Unable to prevent himself, he palmed her breast.

Such comfort in Sarah's company. Who would have thought it? The two of them cast adrift, coming together like this.

"Oh, Sean."

He shouldn't, he really shouldn't take advantage of her. But he'd learned that in life—comforts were few. And the comfort she offered ran so deep.

She pressed her mouth to his and the hunger arose. He lay fully clothed except for his boots and gun belt. Sarah didn't seem to care. She wrapped her arms around his neck and wove her fingers into his hair.

"Sarah—" He tore his lips from hers. "This ain't right."

"Why? Why isn't it? In the past—in the past I haven't always been able to choose who took me. That—*that* was wrong."

"Oh, honey." He succumbed and ran his hands down her back. Cupped her fanny. Drew her in.

"Does there have to be a right and wrong between us, Sean? Does there?"

He thought about that, or tried to. What a blessing, what a gift it would be to have someone—even one person—with whom he didn't have to worry about the right and the wrong, the dark and the light, what should or should not be. Might Sarah be that person for him? But—

"Spend yourself in me, Sean." She rolled away but only far enough to start working on his buttons. His belt. He found himself helping her, the two of them fumbling there in the gloom.

When she sat up and pulled the chemise off over her head, he said, "Sarah, I don't want you to think—"

"Think?" Her hair tumbled around her face as she looked at him.

"That I expect this or anything in return for whatever help I give you."

"Lord, Sean, you've told me so enough times."

It was the last thing she said before she drew him to her naked breast.

****

It promised to be a blindingly hot day. Sarah had once again dressed in her dark blue dress, since it was the most respectable she owned, but it proved far too warm for the morning. The sun beat down on her as she walked to Jenny's house, much as it had that first day when the five of them stood on the platform together.

Like fists beating on the top of her head.

What was she doing? Walking to the home of a friend to check on her? Or going at the bidding of the man she loved to ascertain the welfare of the woman he loved?

It made sense that it could not be simple for her. Nothing had ever been simple. But now—well, it could scarcely be more complicated. She, with Luke to worry about just as Sean clearly worried about Jenny. She understood that. At the same time, she could still feel his hands on her, feel all they had done together a mere hour ago.

Maybe she was going mad. After all that had befallen her, her mind might have finally cracked and broken.

One thing she knew for certain: she was head over

heels in love with Sean Hussey.

And so she walked down the road in the blazing sun to look after another woman.

When Jenny's house came in view, it looked neat and quiet. Sean had waited till the mill was operating before sending her down here, thinking Cyrus would be away, and the place did look deserted. The few people she passed, all headed for town, looked at her curiously.

Would Jenny let her in?

She needn't have worried. As soon as she climbed the little porch and rapped on the door, it swung open. Jenny Withers stood there.

How long had it been since they'd seen each other, to talk to? She'd glimpsed Jenny around town sometimes. And of course when younger, they'd seen one another at school.

Now, though, Jenny's appearance shocked her. Jenny always had the prettiest chestnut curls. Today she wore them scraped back ruthlessly, revealing a face that used to be plump and pretty but now looked stark.

Stark and battered. An old abrasion surrounded one eye, a livid bruise colored the other cheek. Her eyes, wide and brown, stared out like those of some wounded creature afraid to make a sound, and Sarah's stomach did a roll, turning her sick.

Jenny, rather understandably, appeared shocked to see her. She stood gripping the door knob until Sarah said, "Oh, Jenny." And Jenny's eyes filled with tears.

"Sean sent me," Sarah went on quickly. "Can I come in?"

"I don't know if you should. If Cyrus finds out—"

Sarah stepped in and shut the door behind her. the interior of the house felt cooler, but not much.

"Did he do that to you? Cyrus?"

Miserably, Jenny nodded.

"Sean was afraid he would. Jesus, Jenny. Have you put a cool cloth on it?"

Jenny waved her hands helplessly. "I—"

"Come to the kitchen. Is it through there?" The kitchen was bright and sunny, painted a nice yellow. Sarah wondered if Jenny loved her little house. If that was enough to offset what she put up with in order to keep it.

"Sit down. Do you have any ice?"

"No."

Jenny sat at the table. Sarah wrung out a clean cloth she found on the drain board in cool water from the pump and laid it gently against Jenny's face.

"Does that hurt? Did he break any bones?"

"No, I don't think so. He just—just slapped me. It was my fault."

"How was it your fault?" And this injury hadn't been caused by just a slap.

Overlarge brown eyes looked up into Sarah's face. "When he told me—told me what had happened at the mill yesterday afternoon, well, I didn't react the way I should."

"How's that?"

Jenny's lips trembled. "I asked if—if Sean was all right. I should have known better. But the question just came out. I was afraid—well, I was afraid Cyrus had killed him."

Sarah's heart quivered. Did Jenny care for Sean the way he cared for her? If so, she, Sarah, had no chance.

"It set Cyrus off. He started shouting at me. Asking why I should be so concerned for Sean instead of him.

And he hit me."

"Just the once?"

"Yes, because it knocked me down. Clear off my feet. If it hadn't, I don't doubt he would have kept on hitting."

And maybe not stopped.

"The man's an animal," Sarah said, beginning to share Sean's indignation.

"You have no idea." Jenny's eyes filled with tears once again.

Sarah went and wrung out the cloth, stalling for time, before coming back and reapplying it. "Tell me."

"Almost before my head stopped spinning, he hauled me up off the floor and took me upstairs. He—"

"You don't have to say."

"All the while, all the while he was pounding into me he kept saying I was his. *His*. And I'd better not look at another man."

Sarah sat at the table. "Are you all right? Down below, I mean." She knew better than most what happened to a woman—or a girl—when a man forced his way in. Brutalized her.

"To tell the truth, Sarah, I don't know."

"You want to see a doctor?"

"God, no. Think how humiliating!"

"Jenny, you've got to get away from this. Away from him."

"And go where?"

"Anywhere."

"If I leave him, he'll come after me. He's told me so more than once. A woman—a wife—is as good as her husband's property. He can do with her what he likes."

That, yes, was the way of their world. Sitting there

looking at Jenny Withers, Sarah believed it desperately needed to change.

Because a woman like Jenny—she had no one. No real friends or relations to take her in. No one save the man who should protect her but hurt her instead.

No one, except Sean.

Sarah understood it then, what moved the heart of the man she loved. Perhaps standing there on that platform together so many years ago had in some way united the five of them. It was only right that Sean should care for Jenny.

But why, why couldn't he love her, Sarah, just a little bit more? Was it so selfish of her to want that?

She said softly, "Maybe if you leave town, Cyrus won't be able to find you. Sean would lend you the money, I know. Because if you stay here, if you stay in town, whoever gives you lodging will just turn you over to Cyrus again."

Jenny nodded miserably and patted the tears from her cheeks. "Sarah, please tell Sean—tell Sean he can't help me. I appreciate him trying, but I've made my bed and I have to endure it."

"Oh, Jenny."

"Tell him the best thing he can do for me is leave me alone."

Chapter Twenty-Five

Sean stood eyeing the train as it pulled into the station, carrying with it a blasting cloud of steam. He'd come out from Sarah's sweltering room in the Three Feathers because he could no longer tolerate the place. He didn't know how she stood it either and was gladder than he could express that he was getting her out of there.

Sarah.

His eyes strayed to the road that led out of town. The same she'd taken to Jenny's house. Emotions rolled in his gut like sickness. He had such a bad feeling about Jenny, he couldn't even express it.

He had a bad feeling about so many things. Maybe he should never have come back to Clabber Mills, because since he'd returned more had gone wrong than right. So far he hadn't been able to help Jenny the way he'd hoped. He hadn't been able to get back at Bennie Clabber either or, now, Cyrus Withers.

He'd been able to change Sarah's circumstances, yes, but at the same time—

He never should have slept with her, never should have availed himself of that comfort. His eyes narrowed on the train, where a few people disembarked and only two boarded, but he didn't see it.

He saw Sarah's face instead. Wide-eyed and desperately earnest, the eyes reaching, reaching for him. Her need reaching for him also.

Having once given in to the temptation of having her, he should have refused to succumb again. Sarah was her own woman, free to make her choices, worth far more than a tumble in the dark.

But, his mind whispered to him, had she not made the choice to lie with him? Had she not drawn her chemise over her head and pulled him to her? Made blindingly intense, desperate love to him, holding nothing back?

Looking once more up the road, he saw her hurrying toward him. At last.

They met just beyond the station and when he searched her face, his heart fell.

"Sarah?"

"Where can we talk?"

Not her room, which he'd begun to detest most heartily. "Walk with me."

They did, both of them sweating. Town seemed busy this morning, with the train at the station and folks hurrying to and from businesses, and the mill. They walked back the way she'd come and down a side road. He took her elbow as they went—just for the comfort of it, so he told himself.

"Well?"

Sarah glanced into his face, her blue eyes troubled and her face tense. "It was like you feared, Sean. He did hit her last night and—well, worse. At least he only hit her the once, but it knocked her down."

"Bastard!"

"He's an animal. But, Sean, you won't do her any favors by getting mixed up in it. You taking an interest in her—in Cyrus's wife—has already made him angry enough to—"

Sean growled, "He hit her because of me."

"No, because he's a brute. But it didn't help that he thinks—well, that you're interested in Jenny."

He was interested in Jenny. Frustration arose, enough to choke him because his hands were tied. She wore another man's ring, like a brand.

"Maybe I can help her get away."

"I suggested that. She says Cyrus has vowed to come after her if ever she leaves him."

"Then what—"

"Sean." Sarah stopped walking and turned to him. "She asks that you leave it alone."

A new wave of pain beat at Sean. "Leave her—to him? Leave her to her fate?"

"Yes."

"I don't think I can."

Some emotion flickered in Sarah's eyes. "Because you love her?"

Unable to face that expression, held so hard in her blue eyes, he turned away. "Christ, Sarah, I don't know what I feel for Jenny." Or to be truthful for this woman who stood before him. Courageous she was. Hurt and damaged and still able to show him a warmth he'd never known. "Except protective. I feel protective. She can't expect me to stand aside while—"

"Even if that's the best thing you can do for her? Because it won't rile him up. And it won't bring a new danger into her life."

"There must be something I can do."

"I thought about it, Sean. I might invite her out to Mrs. Hamilton's house to live with me. But he'd just follow. Beat down the door. Drag her back."

Sean stood very still. "Then I'll have to kill him.

Free her that way."

Sarah blinked rapidly. "And then what will happen to you?"

"I don't care—"

"And to me and Luke?"

That allowed him to focus on her. "I'll wire more money into your account. All of it. The house—that'll be signed over to you free and clear. Maybe—maybe once Jenny's a widow you could set her up out of my money. Would you do that, Sarah?"

She didn't answer at once. Sean gazed at her standing there in the pounding sunlight with her arms folded across her breasts. Little rivulets of sweat trickled down from her temples, and her eyes—

Well, he wasn't sure what her eyes contained, but it might be grief.

"Sean, I'll do anything you ask of me."

That made him blink at her. Not so much what she said as the way she said it.

What did he mean to Sarah Rupert? What had he gone and done by entering her life, by making love to her?

"Honey," he said softly, "the last thing I want is for you to feel obligated to me."

"So you've said and *said*. And the last thing I want is to see you hanged or in a federal prison for the rest of your life."

"Jenny deserves—"

"Jesus Lord, Sean! We all deserve better than what we got, save maybe Rosalee. Look at us! Milo's signing on to a life of servitude whether he sees it or not. I'll never be a decent woman no matter how much money you give me. Jenny's trapped in a marriage she thought would save her, and you—"

"Me?" he repeated softly when she broke off.

"You're willing to throw away the best gift anyone can get. Life ain't fair, Sean. Anything but. And there isn't a damn thing you can do about that."

"You're wrong." He had to believe she was wrong, that he could in some way make up for the past they shared. Else he didn't think he'd be able to go on. "I've— I've been able to help you, haven't I? And I'll help Jenny too. I swear it."

"Good. Then help her by keeping away. Let life sort it out."

"You just said life's an unfair bitch."

"Listen, I thought you came back to get even with Bennie Clabber?"

"I did." Sean glanced back toward the train station. Maybe he could do that first. Settle Bennie, ruin him, then solve Jenny's problem for her, take her and ride out of town. Put it all behind him. Them.

But what of Sarah? This strong, quiet woman who stood looking at him with her eyes full of agony. Was he supposed to just ride away from her?

"Sean, she's asked you to keep away. You need to respect that."

"All right. I will let it ride for now. I need to go away anyhow for a couple days."

"Go? Where?"

"Indianapolis. Mr. Scaggs says Bennie Clabber's in debt, and I mean to see if I can talk to the men who own that debt. See if I can buy it out from under him."

"Goodness, Sean. You have enough money for that? What exactly did you do out west?"

She didn't want to know. He wanted her to love her

new home, and she might not if she knew it had been bought with dirty money.

He ignored the question. "You say Luke starts school tomorrow?"

"Yes."

"Before I leave I'll get the keys to your house. You can spend some time there, make plans while I'm away."

"All right."

They turned back as one and started for town. "You'll need furniture," Sean said. "There's little enough there. Do you want me to pick up a few things and have them sent out? A kitchen table? A bed?"

She slanted a look up at him and he saw *bed* reflected in her eyes. Suddenly it all returned to him—everything they had done together. He wanted it again, so bad it shamed him.

He would not use this woman as others had done.

"Maybe. Sure. Only if you let me pay for it." Her chin tipped up. "From my account."

"Sure, honey." No need to remind her the money in her account had come from him anyway.

Chapter Twenty-Six

Sarah turned a slow circle in her kitchen, eyes wide so she could catch every feature and every flaw.

Luke had gone to school that morning, not appearing very happy about it, and true to his word Sean had dropped off the keys to Mrs. Hamilton's house before he caught the train to Indianapolis.

No, not Mrs. Hamilton's house. Not anymore. *Hers.*

The flaws, as she saw, were numerous, but so were the features. This, as she could tell at a glance, had been a working kitchen where Mrs. Hamilton and her sister had spent most of their time, and it showed. The heart of the home, it needed repair and cleaning and—and love.

Sarah wanted to keep it the heart of her home. She could scarcely believe she would have the chance. Never in her wildest dreams had she imagined she might own a house.

A home.

She liked the feel of the place. Unlike the Gregsons' and any other house she'd inhabited, it felt friendly. And that meant the dirt and wear didn't matter.

After three full spins with her arms stretched wide, she stopped and let her hands fall to her sides. She listened.

It seemed to her that places always had something for which she had to listen, the way a deer listens while it grazes in the woods. Dangers. At the Gregsons all those years, it had been Mrs. Gregson's voice complaining about something, or Mr. Gregson coldly decrying someone's sins—or worse, his footsteps as he approached her room at night.

More lately, it had been folks talking bad about her, or about Luke. Men in the saloon whose voices carried even upstairs.

Here, there was silence. Blessed silence.

She squeezed her eyes shut and absorbed that. It had been so long that she'd been busy pushing things away from her. Shutting what happened to her into a tiny room. Denying what lay in her heart.

Now her heart belonged entirely to Sean Hussey. And it had brought her—this.

Even if he never loved her back the way he should, even if he decided Jenny was the one he wanted and he'd wait forever for her to be free, even if he went away to Indianapolis or somewhere else and never came back, well she had this quiet, peaceful place.

All she had to do was work and make it into what matched her dreams.

Upon that thought, she drew a pail of water and, hot as it was, fired up the cookstove with fuel from the woodbox. She would begin by scrubbing this room from top to bottom. Put her stamp on it, so to speak.

For the first time ever, she would be working to make something her own.

And, lord, there was a lot of dirt! Not that Mrs. Hamilton had necessarily left the kitchen that way, but since she'd gone, plenty of dust had settled in and turned into grime. The walls needed a coat of fresh paint. She wondered how she could afford it and then thought of all that money sitting in the bank under her name.

Sean.

She would have to be careful with that money, though, because it needed to last her and Luke till she got on her feet and started earning. How much could a lick of paint cost? And what color should she choose?

She thought of Jenny's bright, sunny yellow kitchen and envied it. Don't do that, girl, she told herself. Don't envy anybody else ever again.

She scrubbed until her knees and back ached and her hands turned red. Then she walked through her house again, looking for a place she could spend the night.

No furniture, but she reckoned if she took a blanket from her room at the saloon, when she collected her other things, she could curl up in a corner of the downstairs bedroom and spend the night.

She walked back to town through the heat of the late afternoon and stopped at Rachel's to see how Luke's first day at school had gone. He wasn't saying much, sitting with Danny on the porch munching on cookies Rachel had handed out. She could tell, though, from his expression, that it hadn't gone too badly.

She wouldn't pluck him away from here just yet. Not till she got some furniture, set the house up, made one of the rooms upstairs his alone. But she—she would be out of the saloon this very night.

She visited with Rachel before walking down to the saloon and going in. When she entered, she saw she'd got lucky. Mr. Bracer was sitting at one of the tables with Stu, going over inventory.

He looked a little impatient when she walked up and interrupted them.

"Yes, Sarah, what is it?"

"Mr. Bracer, sir, I'd like to hand in my notice."

"Your what?"

"I'm quitting my place here as a—a hostess."

He exchanged a surprised look with Stu, whose mouth hung open, and said, "But you begged me for this job, more or less."

"Yes, sir, and I'm grateful you took me on to—to tide me over, like."

"You've found another position?" His astonishment wasn't flattering. Who, it said, would hire a whore for decent work?

She flushed. "I'm embarking on a new life, Mr. Bracer."

He looked even more astonished. "Marriage? You found somebody to marry you?"

Sarah wanted to fall through the floor. The few customers at this time of day, overhearing everything, turned their heads to stare.

Gently she said, "I've come back to collect my things." Summoning up what dignity she could, she placed a coin on the table in front of him. "I'd like to buy a blanket off you."

He sat back in his chair and glowered at her. "You're beginning a new life but you need to buy a blanket?"

"Never mind. I'll buy one at the general store." What she should have done in the first place.

But he snatched up the coin. "You know, Sarah, I gave you a chance. And yes, you did bring in some custom. Now you do this to me? Light out and leave me flat?"

Custom. It was her body, not his. "I'm sorry, Mr. Bracer. Things have changed."

"Take the blanket. But don't try and come back, hear?"

It did not take her long to gather up her belongings. She'd never owned much. When she walked out, Mr. Bracer's glare fair burnt a hole through her back.

What would she do if the enterprise she planned didn't work out and Mr. Bracer wouldn't take her back again? Panic fluttered in her stomach as she once more made the long hike out to Irish Road. She had no idea when Sean might return—a few days, he'd said. Or he might not come back, disappearing as mysteriously as he'd arrived.

As she discovered soon after reaching her new home, she'd forgotten to procure a lamp. She used the outhouse when evening fell and then made herself a nest in the corner of the bedroom, the doors locked around her.

She didn't feel afraid here. Even the dark, when it came, seemed friendly. But the house did creak around her as the boards lost the heat of the day. And the blanket smelled like the saloon.

She'd never before realized the saloon had a smell, and she wondered if it tainted her also. If Rachel could smell it on her when she visited. If Luke could. If Sean did. How long would it take her to lose that taint?

She should have bought herself a new blanket. But just like the kitchen, the blanket could be cleaned.

Could her soul be cleaned, though? Cleaned of the things that had been done to her? Of the things she'd done?

She curled into a tiny ball there in the corner of the otherwise empty bedroom and listened to the mice scampering.

Mice. Something else she'd have to take care of here at the beginning of her new life.

Chapter Twenty-Seven

Even after all this time, Sean still hated riding trains. Though trains had, more or less, built his fortune, riding on them was a lot different from holding them up with a set of pistols. Every trip took him back to that first journey, the one that had ended at Clabber Mills.

He remembered how frightened of the train little Rosalee had been when they'd boarded in New York. She'd tried to shrink away and cried so hard, Mrs. Kendall had slapped her, which made Sean mad enough to spit.

Even he, an ignorant Irish lad off the streets, knew you didn't slap someone for being scared, which they couldn't help. In truth, he'd been a bit scared of the snorting engine too, though he'd fought not to show it. He'd been more scared of where they were going and where he'd end up.

Justifiably so, as it emerged.

The trip back to Clabber Mills today should please him. He'd done well, very well indeed, in Indianapolis. Dealing with Bennie Clabber's creditors.

Besides—

He'd awakened in his hotel room this morning missing Sarah. Not just her body, either, although, yes, he'd come awake in *that* condition. He'd wanted the softness of her body beneath him, the taste of her breasts. Even more, he'd missed the look in her eyes when she gazed at him, her hesitant, almost breathless smile. The way she said his name.

Sean.

He missed her.

But he had a lot of business to do when he got back to Clabber Mills. And anyway—

It had been Jenny he'd had in mind to seek out all these years, hadn't it? Not Sarah.

Nothing saying he couldn't help the both of them, and Milo too, if he couldn't talk that young man out of marrying into the very family that had abused him.

As for Bennie Clabber, he had the answers for Bennie now, resting in the pocket of his waistcoat.

That should make him feel happier than it did, the prospect of ruining the man who had made his life hell. As it was, he felt some satisfaction and a measure of wariness. He promised himself the happiness would come.

The train began to slow for the Clabber Mills station, and his stomach muscles tightened. They pulled past Jenny's house—all quiet there—and past the mill where men waited to load a mountain of lumber. He had a few pieces of furniture he'd bought for Sarah. They'd need to be unloaded. He hoped she liked them.

Sarah.

Would she be at the house out on Irish Road now?

The train pulled in and he disembarked, not letting himself think too much about it, and saw Sarah's furniture unloaded. He walked down to the livery and hired a wagon, paid a man to help him load up his purchases—a fine table and chairs, a bedstead and mattress, and a settee that had caught his eye. She'd need more, much more, but she could choose the rest herself.

He would run these things out to her now and deal with Bennie Clabber later. He had to plan that encounter carefully. The where. The how.

Rain clouds gathered overhead. It wasn't as hot as the past few days had been. The surrounding fields burgeoned with green corn and a few curious cows stopped to watch his wagon pass.

When he pulled in to the house on Irish Road, he saw wash hanging out back. The porch had been swept and some of the front flowerbeds tamed.

Sarah, hearing the clatter of the wagon, came hurrying out and stood with her hands on her hips.

A big smile spread across her face. Seeing it, some of the hard uneasiness that gripped Sean's guts eased.

He hopped down from the wagon eagerly. "Sarah! I picked up a few things for the house. I hope they're what you want."

She hurried up, but it wasn't the items in the back of the wagon that held her attention. Instead, she looked at him.

"I'm glad you're back."

"Glad to be here." For the first time in his life, he meant it.

"Did you have a successful trip?"

"Very successful. How's the house?"

A quiet joy took light in her eyes that usually remained so solemn no matter what she was doing. "I love it. I just love it, Sean. It's perfect."

He glanced at the building. Didn't look perfect to him, but then, it wasn't his house.

"That's good, honey. I'm really glad. Want to see your new things?"

"Is that a bedstead and mattress? I've been sleeping

on the floor."

"Well, we can't have that, can we?"

He stole another look at her. Light brown hair piled on her head, half fallen down. Plain clothing unlike what she'd worn at the saloon. Yes, she could almost be a different woman.

"Come see. I've cleaned the kitchen and I'm working on the parlor. I want to buy some paint, but I also want to be careful with the money. You need so much for an empty house."

He followed her in quietly, letting her show him everything she'd done with tangible pride. The kitchen looked a wonder and he told her so, making her glow brighter.

"It smells better, don't it? Sean," she turned to him suddenly, "do I smell like the saloon?"

He gazed at her in surprise. She stood so close he could touch her if he wanted, and he tucked one strand of tumbled brown hair behind her ear.

"What are you talking about?"

"After I got here, I could smell the saloon on the blanket I brought and on my clothes. I've washed them now, but—" She stepped still closer. "Do I stink of that place?"

He met her gaze, beseeching him, and everything within him softened. Much had been done to this girl, to this woman. Some he could help to repair. Some he couldn't.

He leaned over her and took a deliberate sniff. "No, honey. You smell like soap and like—like Sarah." He shouldn't tell her that scent aroused him a little. All right, more than a little.

She placed both her hands on the front of his coat.

"I'm glad."

He wanted to kiss her so bad it hurt. But he didn't want her thinking that was why he'd come here.

"Let's get your furniture inside, see how you like it. We'll probably have the devil's own time getting the bedstead through that skinny bedroom door."

In the end, the mattress gave them more trouble. Sean had shed his coat and they were both sweating before they accomplished the task and set the bed up in the room Sarah had chosen for her own.

"We'll get a cot for Luke, for the time being. When are you figuring on moving him out here?"

"Don't know." Sarah blew another wisp of hair off her cheek. "This is the first week of school, and I don't want to make that any harder than it has to be. The other children make fun of him—because of what I am."

"What are you, besides a mother doing whatever she can to look after her boy?" If Sean's pa had done that after they'd landed in New York instead of drowning his grief over Ma in a bottle, Sean wouldn't have been running the streets. And he wouldn't be here now.

With Sarah.

"I just don't know if I'll ever live it down, being the whore from the saloon."

"You're not that. Never that."

Almost—almost he leaned down and kissed her cheek. If he did, he'd want more. He'd want her lips and her breasts.

So he turned away hastily and grabbed his waistcoat. "Let's go in the kitchen. I want to show you something."

Seated at her new table, he pulled out the documents he'd brought from Indianapolis and spread them on the wooden surface.

"Do you know what these are?"

She peered at them, her face intent. "Some kind of legal papers."

"I've bought up the debt on Bennie Clabber's farm."

"You have?" She looked amazed. "But—I didn't know he had any debt. That farm's always been one of the most successful in the whole district."

"That's what I thought too, but the last half dozen harvests have been poor and he's borrowed. From his brother. And from these men I've just been to see, in Indianapolis. Shit, half the farms in the area are in debt. I could ruin them all if I wanted."

Her gaze met his again. "Ruin them?"

Sean folded the papers carefully. "It's what I intend to do to Bennie. Call in his debt. Destroy him."

Her lips parted.

"He won't be able to pay." Dark emotions rose in Sean's breast. "He won't. And I'll take the farm from him. Don't you see, Sarah? I'll own the very place where he lorded it over me and treated me like dirt." He stared at her triumphantly. "I'll own the dirt itself. It's a beautiful justice."

Chapter Twenty-Eight

Sarah wanted to ask Sean to stay with her that night. She longed to kiss him, to touch him. To invite him to help her christen the new bedstead in the tiny bedroom, even though they had no sheets yet, just the blanket that she'd washed and hoped no longer smelled like sin.

But he had other things on his mind. Business. The business of ruining Bennie Clabber.

Could he truly take the man's farm away from him? If he managed it, that would indeed be a fine justice.

"I have to get the horses and wagon back to the livery," he told her as they stood outside. Dark was just falling, soft and clouded.

"Will I see you tomorrow?"

"Not sure. When are you figuring on moving Luke out here?"

"A few days yet. Maybe on Sunday." She hesitated. "You could stay the night with me before then. If you like."

Before he could answer, before he could refuse, she leaned up and kissed him. What started as a simple pressure of lips on lips soon exploded like a wagon load of TNT. They stood there in the new dark with desire consuming them.

"Sarah, we shouldn't."

"Why?"

"I'm not helping you for—"

"I know that. Will you get it out of your head? If you don't want me—"

"I didn't say that. Sarah, you must be able to tell I do."

She could think of nothing better than having him with her in that little room, in her new bed. But if he had other ideas—

"Is it Jenny?"

"What?"

"Is it because you want her instead? Instead of—of me."

For a moment he went silent. Sarah thought he would not reply.

"I'll be honest with you, Sarah."

"I wish you would."

"I'm not sure what I feel for Jenny. Or you."

Should she tell him she knew what she felt for him? That she loved him the way she'd never expected to love any man. It might provide too much pressure. And if he came to her, she wanted it to be because he wanted her too.

More than anyone else, including Jenny.

"All right." She took a deliberate step away from him. "I'll not hold you, then."

"Sarah—"

"It's fine, Sean. We all of us carry a weight of sorrow. You—me—Jenny. If you'd rather be with her, I'll not begrudge it." It cost her a bit to say that. It cost her more than a bit.

"Sarah, honey, I didn't mean—"

"You take care of what you returned to do. Only—" A new thought hit her. "Where will you sleep tonight?"

He shook his head. "It doesn't matter."

"It does." It did to her.

"Sarah, I've slept rough more times than I can count. One more night won't hurt me."

"Well, take care."

He leaned down and kissed her on the cheek again, a lingering kiss before climbing up on the bench seat and driving off.

She stood till he disappeared from sight, and then some.

****

"Mr. Clabber, do you remember me?"

Bennie Clabber turned from the men gathered outside the saw mill. It was midday and hot enough to fry bacon on the street. Sean had been following Bennie Clabber around town all morning, from the general store to the bank and now to the mill where he stood talking to his brother as the workers filed back in from their noon break.

When Sean called out, his voice a clear challenge, everybody stopped. Sean saw Cyrus Withers, his face still bruised, among the men.

Bennie Clabber no longer looked very intimidating. Hard to believe Sean had once been so afraid of him. Not much above medium height, he had thin hair and small merciless eyes. His face wore a pious expression. But as Sean could testify, his hands were hard, and he never hesitated to use them. His brother, standing beside the open door of the mill, might have been a slightly older edition of the same man.

Bennie Clabber eyed Sean up and down even while Conrad stepped forward and raised his arm. "You—we want no more trouble here."

"I haven't come to make trouble." A lie. "Not my

problem, Mr. Clabber, if you choose to employ wife beaters."

Bennie's eyes narrowed abruptly. "John?"

"No, Mr. Clabber. It's not John. It's Sean."

Bennie's expression changed, shut down hard into the one Sean had invariably seen from him. Disparaging. Scornful. The same way the man might look at something found on the bottom of his shoe.

"John," he repeated in turn, deliberately. "You never did learn."

"I guess you were one hell of a crappy teacher, then." Everyone outside the mill listened, stretching their ears for all they were worth. "But I'm not here to talk about old times. This is business."

Bennie began to turn away. "I have no business with you, not since you run out on me."

"That's where you're wrong." One of the myriad places where he was wrong. Sean drew the papers he'd purchased in Indianapolis from his waistcoat and raised his voice. "This here's your debt."

"My—what?" Bennie spun back around. A flush mounted in his face.

"What you owe on your farm. Fine farm, that. Lots of acres and fields. Good stock. Hard to believe most of it's in hock."

A murmur passed through the listening crowd, and Conrad Clabber's face grew as mottled as his brother's.

"How dare you? Damn upstart! Clear off or I'll call the law."

"Yes, sir, I can clear off if your brother wishes. I just thought he'd like to know I've bought up his debt—a huge portion of it. And I'm calling it in. Bennet Clabber…" He fixed his gaze on Bennie with some difficulty, telling himself he was not the boy this man used to bully and intimidate. Not any longer. "You have till Monday to pay me what you owe. Otherwise, I'm taking your farm."

The color drained from Bennie's face, leaving it bone white. For an instant there was dead silence. Then Conrad began shooing his workers inside.

When the three of them alone remained outside the mill in the pounding sunlight, Conrad stepped up to Sean and growled, "How dare you? You, nothing more than a ragamuffin off the street. After all my brother did for you. First you run away without so much as a by-your-leave, and now you think to ruin him?"

"All he did for me?" Sean repeated, feeling himself go dead cold.

"Fed you, housed you, educated you—"

"You forgot a few other things, Mr. Clabber. He beat me regular. Put the fear of God in me. Swatted me if I didn't move quick enough. Put me out in the fields in all weather. Housed me no better than one of his animals." Sean raised his voice. "Tried to take my name from me—the one my dead ma endowed."

He switched his gaze back to Bennie, who stood like a man poleaxed. "Your reckoning's come due, Mr. Clabber. And so's your debt."

Conrad seized the papers from Sean's hand. "Let me see that."

He perused the sheaf with narrowed eyes before glancing at Bennie, who squeaked at last, "You can't do this. It can't be legal, can it, Conrad? We'll get a lawyer—"

"Get all the lawyers you want, Mr. Clabber. If you can't pay me that sum right there," he pointed to the bottom of the first page, "I have the right to take the farm. Oh, the stock and all is yours. Along with your personal possessions. It's just the land itself and the buildings on it that will be mine."

Bennie stared at him with mingled outrage and horror. "You stinking Irish bastard! You damned savage."

"That's me." Sean grabbed the papers from Conrad's hand. "I'll come out to the farm in three days, at noon. I'll bring my friend." He patted his sidearm. "You can't pay me then, we'll conclude this business."

He made as if to walk away and turned back. "Oh, and remember it's Sean Hussey. Just like on those papers."

He left Bennie swearing in the sun.

Chapter Twenty-Nine

It felt good. Sean couldn't say it didn't. The reckoning with Bennie Clabber had been a long time coming, and it satisfied something deep inside him.

Bennie had not expected that. It had knocked the pious expression right off his face, and that was worth every dollar Sean had spent to buy up the debt.

With the papers tucked safely back inside his waistcoat, he went to the saloon for a celebratory drink. It was early for hard drinking, and Stu gave him a stare.

He sat alone with his whiskey at the table he'd shared before with Sarah, and pondered.

Could Bennie come up with the money in three days? He didn't think so. In fact he was betting not. He'd already borrowed from his brother, and though the mill appeared to be thriving, employing a good part of the town, how much more could Conrad lend him? Enough to bail him out?

If not, Sean would take from Bennie Clabber what mattered most to him.

A slow smile crossed his face. In three days he'd own a farm—the same where he'd labored in abject misery. But—what was he going to do with a farm? Moreover, one that was failing to pay its own way. He hadn't thought farther than this moment—that of victory.

He was no farmer, though Bennie had tried to force it on him. He wanted no part of that life. When all was said and done, though, a man had to accept the advantages that came to him. He'd learned that in life such advantages were all too few.

He supposed he could hire someone to run the farm on his behalf, since he'd sworn never to do that sort of work again. And he could live there—live in the very house where Bennie had lorded it over him.

If he wanted to stay in Clabber Mills, that was.

The thought set him back on his heels. Did he want to stay here in Clabber Mills?

No. That had never been part of his plan. He detested the town and all it stood for. He'd intended to come back, check on the welfare of the four souls who'd been cast adrift along with him, maybe discover whether a future with Jenny might be possible. Jenny, whom he'd always carried in his heart.

A future with her wasn't possible, though. Not unless someone took out her louse of a husband.

Another thought danced into his head. Sarah.

He'd already helped Sarah, hadn't he? Got her out of this den of iniquity. Set her up in that snug little house.

That left Rosalee, who seemed to be doing all right on her own. And Milo.

He finished his whiskey, got up, and left the saloon. The sunlight was so bright it hurt his eyes.

When he walked down to the livery, the owner, who'd got used to seeing him, came out. "What'll it be? Wagon or buggy?"

"Neither. Just a horse, please."

He knew the Bligh farm lay out a ways from the other side of town. As boys, he and Milo might have been separated by an ocean. The only times they saw one another were at church and at school when work on their respective farms allowed them to attend. But the bond of having traveled together on the orphan train endured.

Would the Blighs remember him? Would he be welcome on their farm if he came calling on Milo?

He sweated the ride and started up the dusty lane that led to the Blighs' house with some trepidation. It looked well-kept and quiet, baking in the sun. Somebody worked hard at keeping it tidy, the boards painted and the porch scrubbed.

The front door stood open to catch a breeze, so he knocked at the fancy wooden screen and waited.

A woman appeared, coming down the dim hallway he could glimpse through the door. She had dark brown hair piled up on her head and stood no higher than Sean's nose.

"Yes?"

"I'd like to see Milo Digsby."

"Milo?" She leaned forward and opened the screen a crack so Sean could see her face clearly. A narrow face it was, pale and stark.

Was this Temperance Bligh, Milo's future wife? Sean tried to remember the girl she had been, and failed. She would have been quite young when he left ten years ago and couldn't be more than seventeen or eighteen now.

"Milo's out working."

"Temperance? Who is it?"

Another woman appeared behind the first, hurrying out from what must be the kitchen, wiping her hands on her apron. This one Sean did recognize—Mrs. Bligh whose pinched, narrow features resembled Temperance's enough to brand them mother and daughter.

She paused and glared at Sean through the gap in the screen which Temperance still held ajar.

"My husband's busy and the other hands are out in the field, mister. If you're selling something, we're not interested."

"Not selling anything, Mrs. Bligh."

Her eyebrows rose and she examined him more closely. "Do I know you?"

No. I wasn't important enough for you to notice, back when.

"He says he wants to see Milo," Temperance put in.

"Well, he's not here. He's working." As would any decent man be at this time of day, her tone implied. "What do you want with him anyway?"

"He's an old friend."

She sniffed, a clear opinion of what she thought of Milo's friends. "I suggest you come back when he's not busy."

"When would that be?" Sean fixed her with a cold stare that made her reach out and close the screen door.

"Men here work from sun to sun. Now I'll ask you politely to leave."

There was nothing polite about it. Sean wondered if Milo really wanted to take this woman on as a mother-in-law.

"Maybe I'll just wait in his room. He still sleep in the barn?"

She appeared offended. "The hands have their quarters out there, yes."

Hands. Was that all Milo would ever be?

Mrs. Bligh hurried on. "But I'll have to ask you to leave the property. Milo won't be back for hours."

"Yes, ma'am." Sean tipped his hat.

Mrs. Bligh crossed her arms and glared. Sean left the porch.

Not till he reached his horse did Temperance run after him and ask, "What's your name? I'll tell Milo you called."

"Sean Hussey. Tell him—" Sean studied the place thoughtfully. The fine house. The neat fields. Promised rewards, or shackles? "Tell him I may have a proposition for him."

She didn't like that. He could tell from the way her lips pursed. "I'm not sure who you are, Mr. Hussey, but I should tell you Milo won't want any offers. He's all set. He's going to marry me and we'll inherit this farm one day."

And until that day? Would Digger live in a state not much better than that of the abject misery they'd both known when they were boys?

"Just tell him Sean was here," he bade her quietly. "And I'd like to see him."

"I will, but I doubt he'll have any free time. I don't know who you are or how you make your living"—she eyed him—"but if you've ever worked on a farm, you'll know it takes up all the hours God sends."

"I've worked on a farm."

"Well, then, you'll know Milo hasn't got any time for—for gallivanting."

No freedom at all.

"Don't want to gallivant with him, miss. Just talk."

"I'll let him know."

Sean rode off slowly. He could swear he felt the hard stares of both women as he went.

Chapter Thirty

Following his encounter with the Blighs, Sean had no conscious intention of riding out to Irish Road. It was in the opposite direction back through town, for one thing, and would take him past the Withers place, where he was tempted to stop. A visit there would do nobody any good.

The horse certainly did not take the notion on its own. The poor beast probably wanted to end this trek through the hot sun. But, damn it, Sean wanted to share his victory this day with someone. And, damn it, he wanted to see Sarah.

He found her in her front yard clearing away the weeds and sawgrass. She was hunkered down, no more than a dusty-colored figure amid the garden tangle, when she heard Sean's horse and looked up. Then the sun found golden lights in her brown hair and revealed how her eyes lit up at the sight of him.

"Sean!" She bounded to her feet. "What a wonderful surprise."

He laughed as he swung down from the horse. "You look like a little girl again."

"I feel like one."

She had her skirts hiked up, the better to scoot along the herb beds, no doubt, and no shoes on her feet. She'd unbuttoned the bodice of her dress part way against the heat, and half of her hair had tumbled down.

Sean felt desire rise in a staggering wave. He tamped it down determinedly as he joined her. "You've been working hard." He could see exactly where she'd left off with her clearing.

"Yes, but Sean, look! They're all here. The herb beds, I mean. Mrs. Hamilton's herbs. They're overgrown with the grass and all, but they haven't given up. I bet they've been here for years. Just smell—"

She held out her palms, again like a little girl, and he bent his head for a sniff. The pungent scent of mint rewarded him.

"That means I won't have to replant most of the—"

"Smells nice." She smelled nice. Like the herbs and the soil, and her sweat.

He took her palm in his hand and kissed it.

"Oh!"

He hadn't come here to make love to her. Had he?

He released her fingers. "I was out and about and thought I'd see how you're faring."

"Good." She seemed taken aback by the kiss, and had folded her fingers over it. "It's hard work, but I don't mind. You want to come in? There's a shady spot out back where you can tether the horse."

"Show me."

They walked around the side of the house, Sean leading the horse and Sarah on her bare feet. A tree stood in a small paddock. Sean led the animal inside.

"Come on in. I don't have much to offer you besides water, but I'd sure like a drink."

"Water sounds good."

He sat at the table he'd bought her and she brought a pitcher and cups.

"So, Sean, what have you been up to?"

He told her. He related all of it, including his encounter with Bennie and Conrad Clabber, and his trip to find Milo. She listened in wide-eyed silence and thought over what she wanted to say in response, before speaking.

"So—are you planning on staying in Clabber Mills? If you'll have the farm—"

"No. I don't know. I could sell the farm or give it away."

"Give it away!"

"All I really want to do is deprive Bennie of it. That's what he deserves."

She nodded slowly. "I can see you feeling that way. I can see it would be a great satisfaction to take it from him."

"It's what he values most. You should have seen his face, Sarah." Sean smiled grimly. "He couldn't believe that I—a savage, as he called me—have this over him."

"So, you planned this for years."

"I did. Well, not exactly this. I didn't know I'd have the chance to get my hands on the farm. That fell right into my lap when I was speaking with Mr. Scaggs. Getting his place. I just knew I wanted to make him pay, whatever it cost."

Sarah's blue gaze held his. "To make him pay. And find Jenny."

"If I could."

"Sean, are you in love with her?"

He hadn't been expecting the direct question and it made him sit up straighter. He wondered how best to answer. The truth.

"Like I told you, I don't quite know how I feel about Jenny. I always had a soft spot for her. And I guess, yes,

I carried her with me while I was away."

"I see."

"I want to help her. I want to help all of you who were on the station platform with me that day. You're the closest thing I have to family."

"Do you want a future with Jenny?"

"That's not possible."

"If it was, would you want a future with her then?"

"Sarah, I can't look at the future. I never could—not any farther than the signposts I set up. Complete this job. Reach this point. There's never really been a future for us, has there?"

She shook her head again, sadly this time. "Milo thinks he has a future."

"Living under the thumb of the Blighs, just like he's always done. It's half a future, at best."

"At least he has one. I've been surviving, Sean. From one day to the next, just like you said. But now there's this place."

"I'm glad if it makes you happy, honey."

"This place. And you."

For a full minute he wondered what she meant. Then he was afraid he knew. If she wanted a future with him—

"Sarah, honey, I'm nobody. Nobody for you to—to—"

"You're somebody to me. You're the first man who's ever touched me and I haven't cringed. Even with Ben, who was my husband—there were times I had to tuck myself away when he touched me. You know? Into a deep, secret place. Because it reminded me. Reminded me of what was unbearable. It's different with you. I don't know why, unless it's because—" She stopped abruptly.

He hoped she wasn't falling in love with him. He hoped not.

"Sarah, I'm glad if I gave you some—some pleasure. But I'm not worthy of that kind of regard. You have no idea what I did out west to earn my fortune. I'm not a good man. At heart, I'm still what Bennie calls me, a wild boy off the streets. Strip me back hollow, that's all there is."

"Not all. You care about others. You—"

"No. I care about justice, maybe, because we've seen so little of it. I care about a man beating on his wife. I care about Milo entering a life of voluntary servitude, and I care about the harm Gregson did to you. I wish I could put that right."

She leaned across the table and covered his hand with her own. "You can."

"How?" He searched her eyes. "If you want me to go out there and kill him, I will. It would be—"

"Not that. Take me to bed."

He felt shocked despite himself. Even though the thought had been in his mind since he rode out here. Before that, even. He'd awakened wanting her. But she sure as hell wasn't his to use.

"Sarah—"

"Make me feel, Sean. Make me feel something besides disgust at my own body—or worse, nothing. Do you know what it's like, making yourself feel nothing?"

He did.

"I want to feel the way I do when you touch me. Only you, Sean. Only you."

She leaned still farther across the table and kissed him. The flames came leaping just as they always tended to do when Sarah touched him. He could taste the sunshine on her lips and the tang of herbs. He could taste her desire, and it called up his own.

"Gonna be hotter than hell back in that bedroom," he told her.

"Yes, I promise you it will."

Chapter Thirty-One

Sean was right. The tiny room at the side of the parlor felt like an oven. She went immediately and flung up the sash window before turning to look at Sean.

He appeared uncomfortable. His pale gray eyes held a wary expression, as if he might just back out the door and away from her.

She couldn't give him the opportunity. Because she'd been living for this.

"I still don't have any bedsheets." She gestured to the bed. "I've been making do with the blanket. But I washed it so it doesn't smell like the saloon anymore."

She walked up to him. "Sean, are you sure I don't smell like the saloon?"

"No, I told you. You smell like herbs. Woman."

As if a floodgate opened with his words, he seized hold of her, drew her up against his body. They reached for each other, mouth for mouth, and kissed as if they'd been starved for it. He thrust his fingers into her hair, and the pins gave way.

"Sarah. Sarah, I woke up this morning wanting you."

****

That was all Sarah needed to hear. She towed Sean to the bed and undressed him with hasty hands. He helped her at the end—it was much too hot for clothing, and they both wanted shed of their garments.

A fine body, had Sean Hussey. Long and lean, well-muscled without being bulky, and with a light dusting of sandy-colored hair on his chest. On his chest and lower down. Ready for her, he was.

She'd seen her share of men—more than she'd wanted to—starting with Thaddeus Gregson, though she had more felt than seen him since he came to her in the dark. She thrust that thought away from her. *Not now*.

"Sarah?" Sean watched her face. "Something the matter?"

"No." Not ever, with him.

There was only Sean now. Only Sean and her.

They tumbled onto the bed, atop the rough blanket. She landed uppermost and gazed down into his eyes.

"Sean, I hope you don't mind me on top. It—it reminds me less of—"

He gave her one of his sudden, brilliant smiles. "Sarah, honey, wherever you want to be."

The air cooled a little as the sun began to sink and stopped beating on the roof. A breath of breeze blew in the open window, which as yet lacked any curtains. The room grew dim.

Sarah lay where she'd ended up when they finished making love, sprawled across Sean's chest with one arm wrapped around him. Anchoring her. Anchoring her to him.

Her body still quivered with the aftershocks of pleasure and her mind teemed with thoughts and questions.

She wanted never to leave go of this man.

She liked his body, yes, and that surprised her. Ben—Ben had been a young man, not like the vile Mr. Gregson, and not ill favored. His body had been ropey, covered with dark hair like wire bristles. Though she was sure he never meant to, he'd often hurt her when he'd pounded into her. The men she'd taken upstairs at the saloon—well, better not think of them either.

Sean was different. When he touched her, his hands on her body never hurt, and once the passion lit and she started with wanting him, she didn't even think about pain. She reckoned he was just about the most perfect man who'd ever walked the face of the earth.

As she'd always known he would be. Instinct maybe, but she had always known.

She stroked her fingers across his chest and breathed in the air of the room, which smelled like her and him together. His heartbeat had calmed from its previous gallop beneath her ear, and his skin wore a thin sheen of sweat.

"Sean? I've been thinking."

"Hmm?" He sounded like he was half asleep. Maybe if she held her tongue, he'd stay the night and they could lie like this till morning.

"While you're in Clabber Mills, you're going to need a place to stay."

He stirred a bit as if he dragged himself back awake.

She went on, "I could rent you a room here. Like— like Jenny did." She hated to speak the woman's name. "You could be my boarder."

He said nothing, but she could feel he was awake now. Thinking.

She waited, breath held. She'd reached for so little in her life. She'd let herself want so little, but she wanted this more than she could say.

He spoke at last, his voice a rumble in the near dark. "What about Luke?"

"What about him?"

"Wouldn't be proper, would it?"

"Why not? Lots of women—widows—take boarders."

He didn't say what he must be thinking, that she wasn't like other women. She was the whore from the saloon. People would naturally think—

"Not sure if that would be a good idea, honey."

Her fingers tensed on his chest.

"Your reputation—"

"I don't have a reputation, except as a fallen woman."

"But you're looking to change that, make things better for your boy."

"He'd love having you here. He needs a man in his life."

"God, Sarah. Maybe so, but not me." But he didn't move from beneath her hand. Didn't pull away.

"There's three bedrooms in this house. One for Luke. One for you. One for me. If you were to come down here to my room after Luke was asleep—" She slid her hand lower.

"Sarah. Darling." He kissed her fiercely and now the passion flowed from him. "Is that how you want to live your life? This is your chance. To do it different."

"I want you." There it was, raw truth. She couldn't hide it from him, wasn't even sure she wanted to. If she couldn't own this—what she felt for him—there was no hope for her.

"People would talk."

"It's my understanding people always talk." She had her hand wrapped around him now, the heat of him nearly scorching.

"Let me think about it, Sarah."

"You think. Meanwhile, make love to me. Please." Releasing him, she lifted her hands to his hair and guided him to her breast.

Because it would, it would be making love. Even if he didn't know it.

Chapter Thirty-Two

Against his better instincts, Sean stayed with Sarah that night. Or perhaps instincts were what kept him there. Comforted and comfortable. Wrung dry. Wisdom might make him choose to leave, but he failed to heed that wisdom.

Come morning, she made him breakfast in her newly scrubbed kitchen. He half expected it to be awkward. But the awkwardness didn't hit till she said, "It's Saturday. Since Luke has no school today, I'm planning to move him in here this afternoon."

"Oh." Sean looked up at her, a fork full of eggs halfway to his mouth. She looked like any ordinary housewife standing there drying her hands on her apron, her face slightly flushed and her blue eyes steady. But he knew—he knew by now that Sarah Rupert was anything but ordinary.

The way she'd welcomed him to her bed. To her body. The way she'd guided him to her breasts. The feeling he got when he was inside her.

Like nothing he'd ever known.

"I'd better make myself scarce, then."

"No. I was thinking of asking you for a ride in to town."

"I only have the horse."

She smiled. "Won't be the first time I've rode double. I want to go to the general store, get a few more things before I move Luke in."

"Right. I'll take you, then. But after that I'll let the two of you settle in without me here."

"No," she said again, looking stubborn. "I want him to get used to you being here, Sean."

Sean hesitated. He got the feeling Sarah didn't often fight for what she wanted. She was fighting now.

He laid his fork aside. "Sarah, honey, I won't be here in Clabber Mills forever. Best Luke not get used to me being around."

She flushed. "I know that."

"Come Monday, Mr. Clabber's either going to pay what he owes or hand his farm over to me. After that I'll be able to move in there if I need to."

"You mean to throw those people out of their home?"

"If it becomes my property, yes."

"Where will they go?"

"Darned if I know. Or care."

"The family and the workers—"

"The workers will be welcome to stay if they choose. I'll offer them jobs. I won't be able to run the farm on my own. In fact I'm fixing to talk to Milo, offer him the place if he wants it."

"Milo! But he's set to marry Temperance Bligh. Inherit their farm."

"In due time, yes. If he'd rather a future that's not tied to servitude—"

"Oh, Sean. You're not half shaking things up here, are you?"

"Not half, honey—all the way. I don't know if Milo will accept my offer. Or if he can see that far ahead. In my estimation, he's got blinders on. But it's my experience mean people like Emmanuel Bligh tend to live longer than they deserve."

"True." Sarah twisted her hands in her apron. "Will you truly go there to live if the property becomes yours? Only I thought—" She broke off and Sean saw in her eyes the reflection of all they'd done together last night. The raw, soaring pleasure of it, and the deep comfort.

He wanted more of that, sure he did. But he didn't want to mislead this woman who'd had such a hard path.

"Sarah, it's like I told you. I never planned to stay in Clabber Mills, and once all this is settled I'll have to think again. I just don't know yet."

"So—you'll come and go, will you? Help us—me, Milo, J-jenny—and disappear the way you came?"

"Maybe." He got to his feet. "At least I'll maybe do some good before then. Just like I said, we're as close to family as we're going to find."

She fixed her gaze bravely to his. "No matter if it's days or if it's weeks, Sean—I want you here."

Regret and desire mingled inside him, a troubling mix. "Sarah, the last thing I want to do is hurt you."

"Then stay, Sean, please." She walked up to him, linked her arms around his neck and kissed him. Just like that, the heat leaped up. Sean tried desperately to keep his thoughts in line.

"We'll see, Sarah," he told her when the kiss ended. "You get your boy settled in your new home. Get yourself settled. We'll make a decision then."

She searched his eyes. "All right. Just so long as you know—you're welcome here with me."

Her honesty, and the courage of it, moved him. He had to swallow before he could speak. "I'll keep that in mind."

****

Yesterday's heat should have warned Sean that rain was coming. As they rode into town he could see storm clouds gathering on the horizon. The sun that had shone so brightly into Sarah's kitchen was swiftly being swallowed up. An ominous green-gray color crept over the land.

It being Saturday, the general store was busy. Sean dropped Sarah off there and told her, "I'll stop back for you after I talk to Milo. If you have things to take home, we'll rent a wagon."

She nodded. "I may be at Rachel's—the Everetts, where Luke stays, Just up the way—the yellow house set back."

"All right. Try and keep dry."

He rode on through the other side of town headed for the Bligh farm, straight toward the rain. People stared. It had got around, what had happened in front of the mill. He imagined it also caused some interest that he'd brought the hostess from the saloon to town.

He rode past the saloon and a shudder worked its way down his spine. Yes, Sarah had done what she could to survive. If she never set foot inside that place again, it would be too soon for him.

He reached the Bligh farm just as the first drops of rain smacked the ground. Big drops they were, the size of half dollars to start, and thunder rumbled in the distance.

He knew—none better—that farm workers labored seven days a week. He was relieved to see Milo run out from the big barn behind the house when his horse reached the porch.

"Sean?" Milo didn't look overly pleased to see him.

"Come on into the barn. Bring the horse right in."

It did not take more than a few minutes for the rain to become a deluge. The inside of the barn smelled like hay and horses. Mr. Bligh's team stood in two stalls next to each other. Farther back, a group of milk cows were housed. Milo stared at Sean. He stood in his shirt sleeves, his dark brown hair tumbled and his eyes wary.

"Mrs. Bligh told me you were here asking after me the other day. Can't say she was too pleased about it."

Mrs. Bligh. The woman was to be Milo's mother-in-law. But Sean couldn't imagine Milo would ever call her anything except *Mrs*. Old habits were hard to break.

He eyed Milo thoughtfully. Was that what this place was to Digger? A habit? Had his life become no more than that?

"Wanted to talk to you."

"Come upstairs to my room."

The loft—or rather a portion of it—had been partitioned to make housing for the farm hands. Sean supposed there was nothing wrong with that. He'd lived in the bunk house at Bennie's, little more in truth than a shed. But Milo was now a grown man. Was he willing to accept no more for himself than this?

The partitioned chamber had rough wooden walls and was large enough only for a cot and a chest of drawers. Most of Milo's belongings hung from hooks along the wall. He had a chair that looked like it had been cast off from the house, where he invited Sean to sit while he perched on the edge of the bed.

"Lots of talk about you going around town." Milo's honest brown gaze met Sean's. "Is it true you're trying to steal Clabber's farm out from under him?"

"Not steal. I bought out Bennie's debt, all fair and

legal."

"Bennie has debt?"

"Had. I own it now. He doesn't pay what he owes me by Monday morning, I'm taking the farm."

Milo gave a low whistle. "I don't have to ask why, do I?"

Sean shook his head. "Paying him back for what he dealt out to me is the reason I came back." One of the reasons.

"I don't understand how Bennie's farm could be in debt. This place is doing all right."

"You sure about that? Mr. Scaggs at the land office is the one who put me onto Bennie's being on shaky ground. He said farms in the region are struggling."

Milo shrugged. "The last few harvests haven't been very good. Weather is a farmer's worst enemy." He nodded at the clatter on the barn roof. "We need this rain. But by and large, this year's been better."

So Milo, the little boy off New York's mean streets, had truly turned into a farmer, had he? Funny where life led people. And where it didn't. Farming never took for him, Sean. Milo might have been born here.

Only he hadn't.

"Digger—the thing is, I'm gonna need somebody to run the farm for me when I gain possession of it. I was thinking of you."

Milo's gaze filled with astonishment. "Me? But—Sean, I'm all set here. I've got what I want, what I've always wanted, in sight."

"Have you?" Sean leaned closer. "Have you really? What is it, Milo, you always wanted?"

"Why—" Milo said it as if it were the most obvious of things, as if he believed everybody wanted the same, "a place of my own. One nobody can turn me from."

"And you think you'll have that here, do you?"

Slowly, Milo nodded.

"At what cost, Digger? Your soul?"

"Now listen, Sean. You don't have any right to come back after all this time and start finding fault with my choices, or turning my life on its head."

"That's not what I'm trying to do. It may be a consequence, though, of getting you to see the truth. Do you love Temperance?"

Milo's formerly open expression shut down. Sean had seen that happen before in the past when he'd encountered Milo at school or around town, and it caused him physical pain.

"That's got nothing to do with it."

"I think it does, Digger."

"Don't call me that."

"You want this farm. A place nobody can take away from you. But is it worth trading your future? To Temperance Bligh?"

"The Blighs are good people."

"Are they?"

"Maybe they think a little different than I do. But they're my only choice."

"Not any more. That's what I'm trying to tell you. I don't think Bennie can pay what he owes, and that means come Monday, I'll be holding another choice out to you. You just need to decide what you really want."

Sean rose from the chair and went out, down the stairs from the loft.

Milo never called him back.

Chapter Thirty-Three

"And this is your room with your own cot and all. What do you think of it?" Sarah cast an anxious eye at her son. He'd been quiet since she'd brought him out to see Mrs. Hamilton's house—her house, now. Not like himself.

Maybe she'd have done better to prepare him for this change instead of dragging him out here without much warning.

Now he stood with a faintly mutinous look on his face and doubt in his eyes.

"Why do we have to move here?"

"Because we can. I'm not going to be working at the saloon anymore."

His blue gaze moved to her. "You're not?"

Sarah shook her head. "That's good, isn't it?"

He hadn't said much about the past week, his first back at school. She wondered if the other boys were still giving him grief about her.

"But I like living at Aunt Rachel's."

"I know you do, Luke."

"Why do I have to move away? Why can't I stay with Danny?"

"Well, with you living here I won't have to pay Aunt Rachel for your keep, which will help us a lot. And I'm sure you'll still be more than welcome to spend the occasional night there with Danny. He can come here too and stay overnight."

Luke said nothing.

"After school and on weekends, you can help me whip this place into shape. There's a lot to be done. Painting and clearing out. Working in the garden beds. We're going to be happy here, I promise."

Her boy shrugged. He'd grown so tall over the summer, he'd near outgrown his pants again. Would he be taller than his father? Maybe. Though he had a look of Ben about him, she hoped against hope he hadn't inherited Ben's restless spirit.

There'd been something inside Ben Rupert that caused him a measure of discontent. Or maybe that had been her discontent all the while.

"Why don't we go down to the kitchen? I baked some cookies."

"Do I have to stay here tonight?"

"Won't it be fun? Your own room."

"I like living with Danny."

"Son, I know it's a lot to get used to. But—"

She stopped at the sound of wagon wheels out front and went to peer out Luke's window. Her heart leaped.

Sean.

Had he come to stay the night? Did she want him to?

Yes. Even though it might not be wisest while Luke adjusted to their move.

The morning rain had stopped, the storm moving on eastward, and the sun struggled through low clouds. She watched Sean get down from the bench seat, admiring the way he moved.

By God, she could not help how she felt about this man. There was a gulf, so it seemed, between the way she should feel—if only for Luke's sake—and the way she truly did.

She murmured, "Mr. Hussey's here."

"Mr. Hussey?"

"Sure, Luke, you remember him."

Luke nodded.

"Let's go down and meet him."

Sean stood on the porch when she reached the front door, and gave her a smile. He gifted another to Luke, behind her.

"Morning, Luke. How do you like your house?"

Luke stared at Sean curiously. As he had before, he examined the man from head to foot, his gaze lingering on the gun at Sean's hip.

"I didn't know we were moving out here. Away from Aunt Rachel's."

"Your ma wants a home for the two of you, a real home where you can be together."

Tears pricked Sarah's eyes. If anyone understood such a longing, it would be Sean.

"Did you have your talk with Milo?" she asked him and opened the screen door, inviting him in.

He nodded. "Milo still has blinders on. He's thinking about my offer, though."

If Milo had to be beholden to someone, shouldn't it be Sean rather than a man like Emmanuel Bligh? Everybody had to be beholden to someone.

She did.

"I made cookies. Come in the kitchen. I'll put a pot of coffee on."

Sean gestured at the wagon. "Need to unhitch the horse first."

Sarah's heart leaped. Did that mean he was staying? At least a while.

Sean looked her in the eye. "Horse and wagon's ours. I should say, yours. I bought 'em outright."

"Oh!"

"Figured you'd need a wagon out here. You can take Luke to school in bad weather." He grinned at the boy. "Wouldn't want him to miss class."

To Sarah's surprise, Luke gave a reluctant grin in return.

"I'll pay you back," Sarah told Sean a bit stiffly. "From my funds at the bank."

"No." He shook his head. "You hold on to those. Anyway, this is separate from all that. I'll be using the wagon while I'm here in Clabber Mills. Once I leave, they're all yours."

"Oh." Sarah's poor heart didn't know what to do, rise up or plummet.

"Besides," Sean told her more softly, his pale gray eyes fixed on her face, "the money at the bank's for your future. I don't doubt you'll need every penny."

For a future without him? Sarah didn't say what had begun creeping over her, a conviction. No future would mean much, without him.

"Let me put that coffee on."

She wondered as he followed her to the kitchen whether he'd notice a difference in the room. She'd spent some of her precious funds on a cloth for the table he'd bought her and fabric for curtains, and spent considerable time stitching them. She had a small jug of wildflowers in the middle of the table, and their scent greeted her when she came in.

"Well, isn't this pretty?" Sean said at once. "You'd barely know it for the same room."

Sarah glowed. "It's almost done. I've scrubbed the

walls, but I do want to paint them later on."

"It's a lot of work."

"Yes, but you don't mind so much when it's your own." She put the cookies on the table and hurried to prepare the coffee.

Behind her, Sean said, "Luke, do you want to come help me get the horse settled? She's a mare, and I don't think she has a name yet. Maybe you can think of one."

"Me?"

"Well, sure. She's going to belong to you and your ma, isn't she?"

They went out, and Sarah stood gripping the edge of the drain board, her back still to the room. Was this it? The moment when her dreams ended and real life began? Dreams, as she'd learned, were terrifying things. They came true so seldom and they possessed the power to hurt, to disappoint. For a long time when she had to let strangers have possession of her body, and even when she was married to Ben, it had seemed better to keep from dreaming—from hoping—at all.

But now the dreams had crept in upon her. Come stealing when she let her guard down. Sean—Sean had brought them. They'd burst into glorious existence the first time he touched her.

He said he was going to leave. Oh, he would see her right first. Make certain she had all she needed, for as she began to see, that was the kind of man he was.

Her heart had chosen well.

But he had a ruthless side also. Good as he could be to her, to Milo, to Jenny, he could destroy his enemies.

And then he would leave.

Tears gathered in her eyes and trickled down. She blinked them away fiercely. She had no right to weep.

Only look how much better her life had become.

Sean and Luke appeared through the kitchen window, leading the horse. To her surprise, Luke spoke to the man avidly. She caught his laugh.

A miracle. Luke was even worse than her for letting people in.

She had to pull herself together before they returned. The two males in her life.

She set the coffee cups on the table, still thinking about the perilous nature of dreams. She knew darn well she should eschew them. But if she could have one more—if she deserved one wish—

It would be that Sean might stay the night.

Chapter Thirty-Four

Luke was a fine boy, so Sean decided before the afternoon came to an end. Sarah had done a grand job with him, especially given the circumstances.

He might be a bit standoffish at first, and harbored a tendency to become sullen. But Sean understood young boys and knew the attitude for what it was, a defense.

The boy had opened up to him a little while they tended the mare and settled her in a stall at the sound end of the barn. He'd chosen a name for her—Posey—and pitched in, willing to help with her care.

"Now, you'll need to look after her," Sean told Luke, speaking to him man to man, which was something no one had ever done for him. "It's not a fit job for your ma."

Luke stroked the mare's brown nose. "Ma's had a lot of jobs." His blue gaze, very like Sarah's, moved to Sean's. "Do you know where she worked before this?"

Sean not only knew. He supposed he'd been a customer of sorts. "Yeah. I reckon you got a lot of grief over that at school and around town."

Luke rolled his eyes. "You've got no idea."

"I might. I had a rough start here in Clabber Mills before I went away. I expect you've hid a lot of what's happened from your ma, right? To protect her."

"Well, she gets upset. She would be more upset if she knew what they call me."

Sean nodded. "Well, her working at the saloon has ended now. But I imagine it'll take a time for the label to wear off. You should be really proud of your ma."

"Proud?"

"Damn proud. She didn't like working at the saloon, and she didn't like what she had to do there. It's a sacrifice she made to keep the two of you afloat."

Luke cocked an eye at him. "So why are you helping her?"

"Because we knew each other when we first came here to Clabber Mills. Life was real hard back then, too. Getting spat out together by that orphan train, well, it made a kind of bond. I know how it feels not having anyone in my corner. So I'll help her all I can."

"You must be a rich man."

"I've done all right out west."

"Did you earn your fortune with that six-shooter?"

A curious thing to ask. Sean skirted it with his answer. "Out west, most everyone wears a sidearm. What a man achieves with it is up to him. That's a truth you'd do well to remember."

Luke nodded.

"So do I have your word you'll do all you can to help your ma? In return for all she's done for you?"

"I will."

Sean stuck out his hand. "A man never breaks his word, especially once he's shook on it."

Luke hesitated only a moment before shaking Sean's hand. "I give my word."

"Glad to hear it. That's a load off my mind."

"You care a lot about my ma, don't you?"

"I do, yeah." It shook Sean slightly to realize how true that was.

"Then you can count on me."

****

By the end of that evening, Sean noted that Sarah was behaving oddly. She flitted from place to place around the house, brought forth bursts of conversation and refused to look him square in the eye. By the time she sent Luke up to bed in his new room, Sean knew he'd need to have it out with her.

They sat in the kitchen, it still being the most comfortable room in the house. Sean would have been entirely at ease, had it not been for Sarah's air of distraction.

Once the lad had gone up, he looked at her and said, "Why don't you tell me what's bothering you?"

"Me? Nothing."

"Don't lie to me, Sarah. I thought you'd be happy here in your own place."

"I am happy. I'm happier than I can say to put a decent roof over Luke's head."

"But—?"

"There's no but. I'm grateful to you, Sean."

"I don't want you to be grateful to me. Ain't it enough that most our lives we had things meted out to us? The worst of the food and threadbare hand-me-downs. Never quite enough, but we were expected to be thankful. I want you standing on your own two feet, honey, so you don't have to be grateful to anybody."

"I don't know if I'm strong enough."

He snorted. "I do. Not sure I've ever known a woman stronger than you. Strong enough to endure what you did at Gregson's."

She shuddered.

"To take on what you had to for the sake of your boy

after Ben died. To walk with your head up despite it."

Her gaze met his at last. "I'm not sure my head's been held up very high, Sean."

"Looks that way to me."

"I don't know how strong I'll be if you leave Clabber Mills."

A spear of surprise pierced Sean. He didn't want her feeling that way, though after what had passed between them—

"You'll have to be strong enough," he told her. "What I've given you is just a helping hand. In passing, so to speak."

"But—" Her face flushed. "Once you take ownership of Bennie Clabber's farm, won't you have a reason to consider staying after all?"

"Stay in Clabber Mills? Forever?" Looking at the possibility fairly turned Sean's stomach. "This is no place for me. If I can't talk Milo into managing the farm, I'll find someone else."

"Oh." Her gaze darted away from his. "So there's nothing that could make you stay."

He realized then what she asked. The moments spent in her arms had been special, like none other he'd experienced. And he did think of her almost continually when they were apart.

He shook his head sorrowfully. "I don't suppose I'm the sort of man to settle."

"Not even if you get your own back against Bennie Clabber?"

She must have seen the refusal in his face, for before he could answer she rushed out another question. "If you could be with Jenny, would you stay then?"

Yes, well, that was another matter, one that had

rested in the back of his mind for fifteen years. He'd wondered always about him and Jenny Spinner.

Perhaps—just perhaps, over all those years, he'd made of Jenny someone she wasn't.

"How can I say yes or no to that, Sarah?"

"But—but you won't stay for me."

"Oh, honey. Honey, it's not like that. I hadn't planned on any of this happening between you and me. I didn't come back here for—"

"For me."

He wanted to tell her that Jenny had been a kind of dream, one founded by the boy he had been who possessed so little. One that had sustained him. What she, Sarah, had given him, he'd never expected.

Dreams were hard to surrender.

She pushed to her feet from the table where they'd been sitting. "Tell me one thing. Will you be boarding with me while you're in town?"

"I figured I'd sleep in the barn with Posey."

"Posey?"

"The horse. It's what Luke named her."

She tipped up her chin. "Why not here with me?"

"I don't think it would be good for Luke to see."

"So it's over, whatever was between us?"

Sean didn't want it to be over. He wanted the comfort of her, which went way beyond the physical. But he didn't want to negatively impact her life.

He didn't want her falling in love with him.

As if, he thought bitterly, any woman could ever love him, a boy off the orphan train.

He said, "I'll still pay you board." He dug in his pocket.

"Put your money away. It's no good here and I'll

accept no more of it."

"Sarah—"

"You call me strong, but I'll tell you something, Sean. It's the little things that will break us, in the end."

He sat there at the table as she left the kitchen. He listened to her footsteps cross the parlor as she went into the tiny back bedroom and shut the door. And consternation found him.

Because she was right.

Chapter Thirty-Five

They met at the land office right after it opened on Monday morning. Bennie Clabber showed up with his lawyer and his brother Conrad. That made Sean wonder if Conrad had stumped up the money to bail his brother out once again.

Sean had no one at his side but Mr. Scaggs, who wore an eager expression. Sean wondered what Bennie had ever done to antagonize the land officer, because Scaggs appeared primed to witness Bennie's downfall.

The lawyer, a Mr. Rockwell, examined Sean's papers, taking his time with it. When he finished he looked not at Sean but at the farmer.

"I'm afraid these papers are in order, Mr. Clabber. Mr. Hussey is within his rights to demand payment on your loan."

Conrad Clabber grunted. He fixed Sean with a cold eye. "Would you accept partial payment, John? I'm able to raise near half of it on my own property—"

On the mill? Tempting, and Sean thought about it before he answered. "It's Sean, Mr. Clabber—or preferably Mr. Hussey, to you. I will not accept partial payment." He spoke softly, letting some of the Irish creep into his voice. "And I feel it only fair to warn you, should you put up the mill as security, I will buy that debt also. You don't want to lose the mill to me. It would risk putting far too many men out of work. Those men have

218

families. You don't want to be responsible for that."

Conrad's eyes glowed with rage. "You might pretend to be concerned for the welfare of others—"

"I am concerned."

"Then why are you doing this? Why attempt to ruin a man"—he gestured violently at Benny—"who only tried to help you in your youth?"

"Oh, he did far more than that." Sean barely breathed the words. "Far *other* than that. If you wait while I remove my coat and shirt, you can see the scars."

The lawyer huffed.

Bennie blurted, "Now, wait a minute! You were in need of discipline. A tough boy off the streets of New York, that den of iniquity? I gave you the guidance you needed. Fed you, sent you to school so you wouldn't be ignorant. Took you to church—"

"A hell of a lot of good that did."

"And you want to pay me back by taking everything I own?"

"Yes." Sean took a measured step forward. "I want to pay you back. It's the reason I returned to Clabber Mills."

"That's not right. It's not just."

"There's one justice, Mr. Clabber. Not two—for your kind and the children you brought in to work on your farm. You didn't like that I was Irish, did you? A heathen. A savage. I was also a motherless boy who'd been plucked from everything he knew. Terrified. Alone. Did you show me any concern?"

"Children need discipline, I tell you!"

"Sometimes they do. And they need kindness." He thought of Luke. "Respect. Love."

Bennie's features twisted. "You expect me to love

some rat off the streets?"

"And there it is." Sean raised his hands, palms upward. "That says it all."

"Mr. Hussey," the lawyer declared, "you cannot seize a man's property because he failed to coddle you."

"No, but I can for non-payment of debt. I will expect the deed to be in my hands by the end of business today."

He turned on his heel. There was no more to be said—so he thought.

"John—" Bennie appealed.

He spun. "Haven't you heard a word I said? That's *Sean*. It was always Sean."

He left Bennie, who had an expression of mingled disgust and horror in his eyes.

****

He walked out to Sarah's in the rain, she having taken the horse and wagon to run Luke to school. It was a lengthy plod, and by the time he got there he was wet to the skin, but he couldn't think of any place else he wanted to be.

She opened the door to him and he stumbled in, half blinded as he thought by the rain. Not until she pulled him into her arms did he realize there were tears on his face in addition to the raindrops.

"Oh, Sean. Oh, Sean!"

They sat in the cold parlor and he wept onto her shoulder. He'd never done anything like that before, not even close. Though he could remember shedding tears in his cot back out at Bennie's, mostly he'd been too stubborn and too proud to cry.

Now, though, Sarah clutched him with fierce arms and waited silently for the storm to pass.

Sarah.

The very feel of her, the deep comfort of her presence helped him gather his composure. When he pulled away she let go of him, her expression one of tenderness.

"All right?" she asked.

He nodded. If anyone understood what he felt, it would be her. Or Milo or Jenny—maybe Rosalee.

He mopped at his face. "Don't tell anyone in town I sat here greeting like a big lump. They all think I'm a big, hard man."

"I won't." Her blue eyes searched his. "Did it all go wrong? Did Bennie pay off his debt?"

"He has till close of business today to hand over the deed. I've won, Sarah. It's just—"

"Winning don't feel like you thought?"

"It's good. The feeling's good. Only it doesn't heal what's torn up inside me." And yes, if anyone understood that, it would be this woman.

"Never mind. Maybe time will heal those wounds." She reached up and wiped his face as she might Luke's, but there was nothing motherly in her touch. "Maybe I can help. Sean, let me help."

The kiss came like a life raft in the ocean, and Sean clung to it instinctively. He clung to her, to the warmth she offered, to the kind and gentle woman he knew her to be inside. The flames leaped after, and when they stumbled up from the settle and into the tiny back bedroom, there was no question what would happen.

The rain pounded on the roof while he loved her. *Loved her*. The rest of the world went away while they cradled and sheltered each other. There remained only the sound of the rain, the warmth of her body, and the beauty of the woman she was. Not just Luke's mother.

Not the hostess from the saloon who took men upstairs. Not even the little girl who'd stood on the station platform with him, but something far more.

A spirit as trapped as his own. A warm and generous being who deserved to own the world.

After, when they were spent, he lay in her arms with his face tucked into her neck while she stroked his hair. Thinking—thinking he could stay this way forever.

"How decadent is this?" she asked with a rare note of satisfaction in her voice. "Making love in the middle of the day."

And nobody knew. Nobody knew they took solace in one another. And this deep, deep pleasure. No one cared.

"Thank you, Sarah."

"You're thanking me? For what?"

"For giving me a place to fall."

"Oh, Sean. Oh, Sean!"

He loved the sound of his name on her lips. He used to lie in his cot in Bennie's shed as a boy and try to remember how his ma had said his name. Eventually the memory had slipped away from him.

This was almost as good. No, better, because Sarah was real, here and now, and Sean's ma had become no more than a wraith lost at sea.

He lay there with his eyes wide, thinking—if he'd craved receiving this tenderness all his life, surely he'd craved giving it also. So he slid his hand up Sarah's neck to her cheek and raised his head so he could look into her eyes.

"Sarah, don't ever forget how wonderful you are. Any woman who's courageous enough to give out caring this way after what you've been through— Well, you're a miracle."

Her eyes filled with tears. "And don't you forget you have a place here with me. Always. Day or night, whenever you need me."

He stoked her cheek and kissed her, and the sea where they were marooned didn't feel so wide. "Thank you, honey."

"I know you've got things to accomplish here in Clabber Mills. That you mean to help J-jenny and Milo. Rosalee too."

"Rosalee too, if she needs it."

"And I know you have your plans. But I'd be right pleased if you'd lodge here with me. Not in the barn, but right *here*."

"I'll bear that in mind."

"You see you do." She drew him closer. "Now rest for a time, Sean Hussey."

He did.

Chapter Thirty-Six

By morning it was all over town, the news that Bennie Clabber had lost his farm to the stranger who wasn't a stranger after all, but a boy off the orphan train, grown. Sean could not imagine how it had spread so quickly, except that such scandalous tales tended to. He suspected Mr. Scaggs might have had a part in it, for whatever the reason, Mr. Scaggs had little liking for the Clabbers.

Sean had dragged himself from Sarah's arms, redonned his half-dried clothing, and hitched a ride with her when she went back to town for her boy in the afternoon. He had in fact switched seats with Luke outside the school, and the boy had given him a big smile.

He had some thinking to do about Sarah and Luke. Business first.

They'd all met again at the land office where Bennie stood by silent while the lawyer handed over the deed to his farm. A rush of satisfaction came then.

After the others left the land office, after Sean had—very generously, he thought—given Bennie three days to clear off his property, Mr. Scaggs spoke into his ear.

"I'd watch my back if I was you, Mr. Hussey. You're not going to be the most popular man in town during the days to come."

Yes, and that had got him thinking also. What would

happen to his property, to all his money, if someone waylaid and murdered him? He needed to see a lawyer in Indianapolis most likely, and he needed to do it quick.

Meanwhile, he'd returned to Sarah's, renting a horse this time for the sake of expediency. He'd taken up her offer of lodgings, not quite able to convince himself that wasn't where he should be. He needed to sort it all out. Living this way wasn't fair to anyone.

By Tuesday morning, he was the center of attention as he walked Main Street to the bank. Women gazed at him and as quickly looked away again. Men took measured stares from the corners of their eyes. He caught a few whispers.

"That's him."

He'd never been welcome in Clabber Mills, not when he'd first stepped off the train and not now. He must be mad to buy up property here.

At the bank, he arranged for more money to be wired into Sarah's account. He also opened a second account in his name with funds earmarked for Jenny and for Milo, if he needed them.

Then he rented another horse and rode back out to the Blighs.

His reception differed this time. Mr. Bligh himself came to the door, an angry, aggressive expression on his face.

"You're not welcome here," Bligh greeted Sean, proving his recent assumptions. "So you can just turn right around and ride off again."

Before Sean could reply, Digger appeared from around the side of the barn. "I'll take care of this, Mr. Bligh," he called.

Bligh turned on Milo. "He's not wanted here, Milo,

and you'll heed me on this."

Milo hesitated. Sean suspected he heeded Bligh on a regular basis. He could glimpse Temperance standing behind her father, peering out to see what her fiancé would do.

Milo said quietly, "He's my friend, Mr. Bligh. I just want a word with him."

"It's my opinion you should choose your friends more carefully." Mr. Bligh slammed the door shut with considerable force.

Milo's expression didn't change. "Come on up to my room," he bade Sean.

They climbed the ladder stairs in silence. Once in the small space Digger called his own, Sean turned and said, "Well, Digger? I've come for your answer. The farm's yours to manage if you want it."

Milo didn't speak at once. He raised both hands and forced his fingers through his curly hair. "Been hearing a lot about you. You ain't the most popular man in Clabber Mills right now."

"I know it."

"Folks are worried."

"Worried?" That surprised Sean. "About me?"

"Well, sure. You show up here, one of the rats from back east, with all kinds of money. Buy one of the biggest farms in the area out from under a family who founded this place. An institution. People are asking who you're going after next."

"Nobody else. Just Bennie. Though I'll admit I'd like to take Cyrus Withers down."

Milo looked at him. "For Jenny's sake?"

"For Jenny's sake."

"What about Sarah?"

He'd like to take Thaddeus Gregson out too, for Sarah's sake, but he couldn't tell that to Milo. "I've helped her all I can. Got her out of that pestilent place. Gave her a new start."

"That all it is, with Sarah?"

Sean shook his head. His feelings for Sarah were so complicated he barely understood them. He said, "Digger, I'd like to help you too. I've set up an account at the bank to finance Bennie's farm. They'll be out of there day after tomorrow, and it's like I told you before—I'd like you to move in. Run the place for me."

"Why don't you run it yourself?"

"I'm no farmer."

"What about my place here?"

"What place?" Sean spread his hands. "This hole of a room in the barn? Digger, we've talked about this."

"Yeah, we have, and you don't seem to have taken my point. I've worked for this place, Sean. Sweated blood for it. Even if you sneer "

"I'm sure as hell not sneering at you. Far from it. You did what I couldn't—stayed and stuck it out, faced up to the lot you'd been given. Tried to make something of it. I admire that. But—"

"As soon as Temperance and I are married, after this next harvest, I'll move into the house."

"Do you love her?" Sean challenged, even as he had before. "Or is she just a way to step in?"

A battle light shone brightly in Milo's dark eyes. He fought the battle for an intense moment before he asked, "Do you love Sarah? Word is you've moved in with her."

"To tell you the truth, I don't know what I feel for Sarah. Anyway, that's different."

"How?"

"I'm not trying to be with her in order to get something in return."

"Is she?"

Sean's jaw dropped open.

"You've set her up in that house, her and her boy. Been spending nights there, so I hear. The Blighs say—"

"The Blighs know nothing about it."

"They say it's no different than what she was doing at the saloon."

For the first time in his life, Sean wanted to sock his friend. To bang his fist into Milo's face with satisfying force. Somehow he kept from doing it.

"That's why Sarah's treated the way she is," he spat. "Because of sanctimonious fools like the Blighs."

Milo took a stance. "I'm gonna have to ask you to leave."

Sean stared. "That mean you're turning down my offer?"

"It does."

"Digger, it's a good opportunity. That farm's a plum, and you know it. Just needs a good hand at the reins."

"And what would it make me if I took you up on this offer? I'd be a pariah like Sarah. Like you. Besides—I don't have much, Sean. You've pointed that out. But I do have my loyalty to the people who raised me. Can I turn on them now?"

Sean studied his friend for a moment before some of the anger inside him died. "No, if you feel that way, then I suppose you can't. I'll try and find someone else to manage the farm. But if you change your mind, if at any time you decide to leave here, there'll be a place for you."

Digger nodded.

"I mean to offer Jenny the same. If she wants to get away from her brute of a husband, she'll have a place to go."

"I know you mean well. And none of the five of us ever had anywhere to turn, did we?"

"No."

"But, Sean, people don't always appreciate someone coming along interfering in their life. Thinking they know better than the person who's living it."

"That's not what I'm trying to do."

"Isn't it? You're gone from here ten years, more or less. You come flitting back and turn everything on its head, all while saying you don't mean to stay."

Sean said nothing.

Milo stared him in the eye. "Are you being fair to Sarah? I know you've given her that house and you think you're helping her, but I hope you won't forget the most important thing in all this."

"What's that, Digger?"

"Her heart."

Chapter Thirty-Seven

Sarah glanced out her front screen door for the dozenth time that morning, hoping for a glimpse of Sean. The air hung still and breathlessly hot, with thunderheads gathering in the west. She almost wished the storm would break and clear the staggering heat.

She wished Sean would come.

He'd spent last night in her arms. Up till then he'd kept to the barn, away from her, likely for Luke's sake, for he wanted her boy to think well of her. But last night after Luke was asleep he'd come to her bed on silent feet and they'd made quiet love there in the dark.

She'd known then, while holding him to her, while holding him inside her, just how much she loved Sean Hussey.

Maybe she always had, since that first day they'd stood on the platform together, gazing at an unimaginable future.

This morning he'd gone to take possession of his farm. He'd ridden out dressed in his best suit and said he should be back before noon. When he returned, Luke being at school, she intended to take him to bed. Because she still didn't know about the future, but the *now* could be here, in her hands.

She went back to cleaning the front parlor, working in that room precisely so she could keep watch, and the feeling grew upon her. Moment by moment and minute by minute it did, until another hour had passed.

Something was wrong.

When an hour past noon had come and gone, her hands were shaking too badly to do any scrubbing, and a sick feeling had implanted itself in her gut. He should have been back by now. Long since.

She tried to reason herself out of it, thinking he might have gone back to the land office after, or stopped to see Jenny. Even that, in Sarah's view, would be better than this terrible conviction.

That some great harm had befallen him.

When she gave up trying to reason and went out to hitch up the wagon, the thunderheads had closed in and a small fitful wind tried to tease her hair from its bun. It was going to storm. She had to reach Bennie's farm first.

Her hands still shook so bad she could barely hitch Posey to the traces. They started off with a rattle, leaving a trail of dust, Sarah fighting down her panicked emotions.

As she rolled along, her uneasiness intensified. When she passed the Withers house and saw Jenny out front on her knees in the garden, she drew up long enough to call, "Jenny—come aboard!"

"Where are you going?"

"To Bennie Clabber's. Sean's there and I think something's gone wrong."

Somewhat to Sarah's surprise, Jenny climbed onto the bench seat beside her. The two of them weren't exactly friends, but there was a bond, a fierce one, born of standing on that platform together so long ago.

Jenny's hands and the knees of her dress were dusty. She wiped the former on the latter before she said, "What makes you think something's gone wrong?"

"I feel it. Here." Sarah pressed a hand to her stomach. "You must know what's going on. Sean's taken the farm from Bennie Clabber."

"Yes. Cyrus hates him—Sean, I mean. Because he attacked him for hitting me."

Sarah glanced at the woman who sat beside her. Faint yellow bruises marked her face, visible in the queer light. "He does that pretty often doesn't he, Cyrus?"

"Yes."

"Then, Jenny, you have to leave him. You're worth more than—"

Jenny's lips tightened. "Says the woman who's been taking strange men to her bed."

It felt like a slap. So intent was Sarah on her panic, she barely felt it. "Thaddeus Gregson started coming to my bed, started using me that way, soon after we arrived here in Clabber Mills. It went on and on till I married Ben in order to get away. I learned to blank it out—to shut a door on what was happening to my body. That's what I did with the strange men, as you call them."

"Sarah!" Jenny stared at her, open mouthed. "By God! I never knew."

"It was a secret. That's what happens when people keep secrets. If you keep it a secret, what Cyrus is doing to you, it won't end well."

Jenny wound her fingers together in her lap and said nothing.

"Sean will help you get away if you let him." Sean might even claim Jenny for his own, and at this moment Sarah barely minded that. So long as he was all right.

Thunder rumbled overhead as they turned up the long track to the Clabber house. Gray clouds slid past one another overhead like boulders grinding, and rain dashed into Sarah's face. In the murky light, the big white house looked strangely deserted. Windows blank as staring eyes. Barn door gaping open to one side.

"I don't think there's anyone here," Jenny said. "And it's going to storm. I hate lightning storms."

Sarah could feel the electricity in the air, as if the whole world held its breath, and it made it hard for her to breathe in turn. She couldn't see Sean's horse—the one from the livery—anywhere. Had he left here after his meeting? Had everyone gone? What about Mr. Scaggs from the land office?

"Let's knock on the door," she told Jenny. "Just to see."

"All right, but if Cyrus finds out I'm here instead of at home where I'm supposed to be—"

She didn't finish the thought. They both climbed down from the wagon and ran to the porch of the house, raindrops striking ever faster.

No one answered Sarah's knock and the door creaked open beneath her fist. The interior of the house yawned with shadow as she stepped in, Jenny close behind her.

"Sean?"

She could see where the furnishings of the place had been hastily gathered and moved out. A few items, no doubt deemed worthless, had been left behind. A scatter rug in the hallway. An empty bucket. More things left in the kitchen beyond. Bowls and a few dishes, an empty crate meant to be used for packing. It felt oppressive and almost menacing.

Thunder rolled overhead, rattling the windows. Sarah thought of poor Posey, outside.

"He's not here. Let's lead the horse into the barn and

wait for the worst of the storm to pass."

"What'll you do then?"

"I don't know." Find him. But where to look?

Rain pelted down as they went back outside. One of them at either cheek, they led the horse across to the open barn with the wagon rattling behind.

The barn was a fine one, big and with close-fitted boards, and a gable roof. The stock had been emptied from it. Sarah wondered where Mr. Clabber had taken them. The center lane was big enough for the horse and wagon.

"Shut the door," Sarah bade Jenny and deeper gloom enfolded them. It wasn't till thunder once more boomed and lightning lit up the place, streaming eerily between the doors, that Sarah saw what lay further down the open lane.

It looked like a pile of clothing. A coat flung there on the straw-strewn floor.

Sean's best suit coat.

It took a number of heartbeats for her to grasp the truth. When she did, she flew to the pile and went down on her knees so hard she felt the impact in her teeth.

"Jenny! Jenny, he's here... Sean!"

Jenny came and hunkered down at Sean's other side.

"By God, Sarah! Is he dead?"

Sean lay on his side, sprawled with his arms flung out in front of him and his eyes closed. His face, in profile, looked near unrecognizable, covered with abrasions. Beneath the blood, the scrapes and cuts, his freckled skin was as white as that of a dead man's.

Sarah's world abruptly slowed so she could feel her every heartbeat. This could not be. It could not happen to her, not this, of all things. She'd just found him. Only a fate as cruel as any she'd ever known could take him from her again.

She could not hear her own voice for the pounding in her ears and the thunder overhead when she called to him. "Sean?"

"Turn him over onto his back. Careful, now."

It was Jenny who reached out tenderly.

"He may have broken ribs."

Two pairs of gentle hands worked together to turn Sean flat onto his back. A groan broke from his lips. Despite the pounding in Sarah's ears, it was the sweetest sound ever. "He's alive."

"Not by much. Sarah, he needs a doctor. He's breathing, but you can hear the air whistling in his chest." Jenny unbuttoned the shirt from under Sean's chin. "Looks like they beat him pretty good. And they must have taken that sidearm he wears."

"Who did? The Clabbers?"

Sean's lips parted. Another sound issued from between them.

"What? Sean," Sarah leaned closer. "What is it?"

Jenny lifted up her head and looked into Sarah's face. "That was your name." She climbed to her feet. "Somebody has to go for the doctor. You stay here with him while I go."

"But—you're scared of the storm."

Jenny's eyes brimmed with compassion. "And he wants you here with him. You just keep holding onto him, hear? I'll be back as soon as I can."

"Jenny—"

"Sarah, you'd never forgive yourself if he passed while you were gone. And neither would I."

Sarah barely heard Jenny open the door and back the

horse and wagon from the barn. She took one of Sean's hands in hers and gripped it hard.

"Sarah?"

"I'm here, my love. I'm here. You just hold hard onto me."

Chapter Thirty-Eight

Sean rode the train once again, a boy of no more than eleven, dressed in ill-fitting pants that were too short for him and a third-hand jacket, his stomach full of nausea caused by fear and uncertainty. The thumping of the rails came up right through the bottoms of his feet, each thump taking him farther from all he knew and into the unknown.

Already he'd left the wild green hills of Ireland and the ship where his ma had slipped from his grasp. He'd traveled west, and now he traveled west again. Farther and farther from her.

If he continued traveling west, as relentless as the beat of the rails under his feet, would he eventually forget Ma's face? Forget the way she'd looked at him and how she'd said his name? *Sean.* Would he forget the love?

No, because love spoke his name once more.

"Sean."

All at once he stood on the platform, on that fateful day—the five of them in a row. His left hand clutched that of Sarah, beside him. Then came little Rosalee, forgetting to cry at the moment, though she'd cried endlessly for her mama up to now. Then Jenny and Digger on the end, all holding hands.

The five of them were all they had. He couldn't abandon them, he couldn't—

A wagon rattled up and a man with hard eyes

stepped from it and onto the platform. Stared Sean in the face.

"Is this him?"

Bennie Clabber reached out and swatted Sean. Hard. The impact knocked Sean's hand from Sarah's and turned him around.

Suddenly the searing bright sunlight on the platform faded. Flickered. He was surrounded by men, all striking at him. Bennie Clabber, he with the cold eyes, struck hardest.

"Sean? Sean, hold on to me. Help's coming."

"Sarah?" He opened his eyes and her face swam into view, looking different somehow. Older. All the innocence flown.

But he saw so much love in her eyes it fair made up for everything.

"Sarah, it was you all the while. It was you who had hold of me."

"Always, Sean. I loved you always. And forever, I will."

****

Jenny did stellar duty and brought not only the town doctor but the marshal, who'd happened to be in town when she got there. The storm had passed by then and a bright wedge of gold showed in the west, though the clouds in the east still looked black as ink.

By then Sean had come to himself and remembered what had happened to him, there in the barn. Sarah had some trouble keeping him from trying to get up, while waiting for help to arrive.

"Sean, you're busted up bad. Jenny's bringing help."

"Jenny is? What's she doing here?"

"Does it matter?" Sarah leaned down and kissed

him, which rendered him still. "You listen to me, Sean Hussey. You're gonna have to stay put till—"

"Say my name again."

"Sean Hussey."

He gazed into her eyes. "Again."

"Sean."

"Ah, God, Sarah!"

"What is it? What?"

He clutched her hand hard. "Don't leave me. Whatever happens, don't—"

"I'm not leaving you, darling."

When the others came, she found it hard to keep her promise. Doc Andrews wanted to transport Sean to his office in town. Sean, who wanted to talk to Marshal Buttrey, turned stubborn instead.

"I was here to take possession of the property," he told the man through wheezes that Doc Andrews said indicated he had broken ribs. "They were waiting for me in here and jumped me from behind as soon as the papers were in my hands. I drew my gun and had time to take one shot before they wrestled it away from me. You'll find the slug in the door over there."

"Who was it jumped you?"

"Bennie Clabber, his brother, Conrad, and a number of Bennie's hands. They took the deed back. It fell on the floor when they hit me, and they snatched it back."

Marshal Buttrey said, "We'll worry about that in a while."

"Mr. Scaggs at the land office knew I was taking possession today. He can testify—"

"He wasn't here with you?"

"No, not today. But—" Sean wheezed harder.

"Never mind, I'll catch up with him and get his side

239

of it."

"Mr. Hussey," said Doc Andrews flatly, "you're lucky to be alive. If these two women hadn't found you when they did," he nodded at Sarah and Jenny, who stood side by side, "I hate to think how you'd have fared. I'm taking you to my office."

"No." Sarah spoke up clearly. "You'll take him to my house instead. Out on Irish Road."

There had been far too many times in the past when she hadn't spoken up as she should. When she was afraid. Or knew she wouldn't be heard—or believed.

But the men heeded her now. They loaded Sean up with care, Sarah doing her best to stay within his reach all the while.

Marshal Buttrey said he'd ride back to town, see if he could locate Mr. Scaggs. Follow up on the assault.

Sean croaked at him, "You see you do. Hope Scaggs is all right."

Doc Andrews declared he'd follow them out to Sarah's house, where he could patch Sean up.

Jenny sidled close to Sarah. "Can you drop me off at home on the way?"

Sarah eyed her. "You going to be in trouble with Cyrus over this? Everybody in town will know you had a hand in rescuing Sean."

"I don't know." Jenny's big brown eyes looked anguished.

"You're welcome to stay with me if you need a place."

"If I leave him—Cyrus, I mean—it's over, Sarah. I can't go back."

"Would that be such a bad thing?"

"I don't know if I'm ready. Sarah, I'm not brave like

you. I don't know if I can step out on my own."

"Land sakes, Jenny. I'm not brave."

"You are so. And he—" she nodded at Sean, being settled in the bed of the wagon, "is lucky to have you."

"Well, Jenny, if ever you want to leave that husband of yours, you have a place with me. Understand?"

"I do. I'm grateful."

No sooner did they drop Jenny off and get Sean settled in the house on Irish Road than Luke got home from school and Sarah had to make explanations all over again.

Luke's eyes grew round. "Is Mr. Hussey going to be all right? I like him, Ma."

"I do too. In fact, he's going to be staying here while he recovers. Maybe—" Sarah drew a breath. "Maybe longer."

"Longer?"

"We'll see." She didn't want to make unfounded assumptions. "Son, can you run out and look after Posey? I haven't had time, and she's had a real hard afternoon."

Luke went with alacrity.

Sarah slipped through the parlor to the room where the doctor tended Sean. Pacing in the doorway and looking in, she had to smile. "Doc, by the amount of swearing, I gather he's going to be all right."

Doc Andrews grunted. "Good thing you're young and strong, Mr. Hussey. You're going to be hurting for a while. And your head took a good thumping."

"Won't be the first," Sean muttered.

"Seems you've got you some enemies here in town." The doctor glanced at Sarah. "And some friends too. You going to be looking after him, Mrs. Rupert?"

"I will."

"Well—ah—keep him quiet if you can. No—er—strenuous activities."

"I'll definitely bear that in mind."

The doctor finished what appeared to be painful bandaging and went out, carrying his bag. Sarah sat down on the side of the bed.

Sean scowled at the door. "The old fart. Is that all he thinks you're good for? Strenuous activities?"

"Don't get yourself all in a twist, Sean."

"Why not?"

"It isn't good for you in your present state. And anyway, he's right."

"He isn't."

Her gaze met his indignant one. "I'm the town strumpet, remember? Are you sure you want to stay here and besmirch your reputation?"

"I'm sure. Sarah—" He reached for her hand. "I need to tell you—"

What did she see in his eyes? A load of anguish. Did he want to tell her he couldn't—wouldn't—stay in Clabber Mills, not for any reason? Especially after being beaten at Bennie's hands once again.

She couldn't bear to hear it.

"Not now," she told him. "You just concentrate on feeling better. On getting that deed back again. Anything we have to say can be said later on. Right?"

He nodded, but the storm of emotions remained in his eyes.

Chapter Thirty-Nine

When two days had passed, Sean had to accept the fact that Sarah was avoiding him. How that could be so—how a woman who was almost continually in his company and fussing over him could also avoid him, he could not say.

Maybe the simple truth was that she avoided conversation with him. Meaningful conversation, anyway, beyond *Would you like another cup of broth?* And *Are you comfortable?* Because she did care for his every need. Brought his meals and talked him round if he got restless. Listened to his cussing when he tried to move.

When he woke after a sleep, or even a doze, she was always there at his bedside. And she inevitably hurried up and went about some task before he could find the words for what he had to say.

At each point in the day when they might be alone, when he fought to order his thoughts once again, she would decide his scrapes and cuts needed cleaning or he would have some caller.

He had a lot of callers.

The doctor came back regular. The marshal came to say Mr. Scaggs had been found at the land office with his head bashed in. He had been tended in turn, and told the story of how Bennie and his hands had come in and sought to silence him permanently. As for Bennie

Clabber, the marshal had spoken with him. He'd denied everything, but the deed had been found in his possession, as had Sean's gun in the possession of one of his farmhands. Under strict questioning, Bennie had cracked and admitted to the attack, while declaring it was only right he should chase off the dirty Irish varmint. The farm was his—and no one but he should live upon it.

"Gonna be a hard pill for him to swallow," Marshal Buttrey said, even as he returned the deed to Sean's hands. "The place is yours now, Mr. Hussey."

Sean didn't care how hard it was for Bennie. It had been a hard pill for him to swallow also, that Bennie Clabber—he with the hard hands—had beaten him down once more, and him a grown man who had sworn such a thing would never happen again. Despite the fact that Bennie had been apprehended—and it had taken the marshal a number of companions to achieve the deed— it rather put a dent in Sean's pride.

Jenny and Milo both came to see Sean there in the little room off the parlor. Jenny had a few new bruises, but she refused to talk about them. She also refused to look Sean in the eyes. Even when he reiterated that he was willing to help her out financially if she needed, and that she could stay at the farm now he held the deed to it, she merely dropped her fine brown eyes to her hands, clenched in her lap.

He supposed she wasn't ready to make a change in her life, and you couldn't force a person who wasn't ready. So he didn't tell her that one of the accounts at the bank was earmarked for her. Time for that later when she needed it.

Milo came quietly with his straw hat in his hand and a somber look in his eyes. He sat in the chair beside

Sean's bed, bringing in the smell of the outdoors, and sunshine.

"I'm sorry for what happened to you, Sean. Truly I am. I hope that even though I've turned down your offer to run Bennie's farm, we'll still be friends."

"Sure we will." Propped on the pillows and feeling stronger, Sean regarded this boy turned man. "You've turned me down for certain, then?"

"For certain, yeah. The Blighs have been good to me in their way."

They hadn't, but if Digger's mind was made up, Sean wouldn't argue it further.

"And," Milo looked troubled, "it's coming up on harvest. I can't abandon them at the busiest time of year, can I?"

Milo clearly was a man whose loyalties ran deep. Sean couldn't fault that. But he said, "And after the harvest comes your wedding. You sure that's what you want? To be tied to Temperance Bligh for the rest of your life?"

When Milo's gaze returned to Sean's, it was troubled. "I'll admit I don't love her. And I reckon she don't love me. But where would a fellow like me"—he lifted empty hands—"find someone to love him anyway?"

Something inside Sean cracked and melted—melted into pity and longing. "You're right, Digger. Love's a rare thing. But an empty marriage is no prize. Just look at Jenny."

Milo nodded. "You going to be staying here in Clabber Mills when all's said and done?"

Sean shook his head. "Well, that remains to be seen."

Sarah listened to all this, or bits and pieces of it as she came in and out of the room, an unreadable look in her eyes. She wouldn't stay put long enough for Sean to talk to her.

So one sunny morning when the house was quiet, he got up, struggled into a shirt and some trousers, and made his way out from her bedroom.

He found Sarah in her big, scrubbed kitchen fussing at the bench on the back wall, her light brown hair pinned up so only a few tendrils fell against the tender nape of her neck. She wore a plain, often-washed gown and a sack apron. When she turned at his step and her blue eyes went wide, he thought she was just about the best thing he'd ever seen.

"Sean! What on earth are you doing up?"

"Looking for you."

"Oh." She didn't appear particularly happy about that. Doubt invaded the wide eyes and her lips tightened.

"Sarah, honey, we need to talk. I want to talk. And since you won't stay put long enough in that room—"

She turned to face him, putting aside the bunch of herbs she must have brought in from the partially cleared garden. Their scent arose in the room. Dill.

She tipped up her chin in a gesture that had become familiar to him. "I don't suppose I want to hear what you have to tell me, Sean Hussey."

"Why?"

"I reckon you'll tell me you've decided to leave Clabber Mills. And I—" Her eyes widened farther. "I don't want you to go."

He took a step closer. Everything within him longed to touch her—to trace a finger along that delicate neck. To caress her tensed shoulders. But first, words had to be spoken.

"You think that's what I want to say to you? That I'm leaving?"

"Isn't it? You hate this town. And now that you've fallen foul of Bennie Clabber again—"

"Bennie's a small man. I'm not afraid of him." He declared it to himself as much as her.

"Maybe not. But you can't deny that from the moment we got off that train, you've wanted to be anywhere else."

It was true. He detested Clabber Mills. But he'd seen a good portion of the world and he knew he had no home out there anywhere.

He took another step toward her. "You're forgetting something important, Sarah."

"That you own property here now? I reckon you can find somebody besides Milo to manage that farm."

"Not that."

"Then what?" She tipped her head.

"You're here."

He completed his journey and caught her shoulders between his hands. "You're here, Sarah, honey. So how could I ever leave?"

He kissed her. He made it soft and sweet, trying to say all the things words could not, and he felt the pieces fall into place inside him. She, Sarah, not a place—was his home.

"Sean." When the kiss ended she clutched him hard. Hard, without regard for his bruised ribs. He buried his face in the soft skin of her neck, and inhaled.

"I love the way you say my name. Say it again."

"Sean?"

"That's it, Sarah. I have to tell you something. I

came back to Clabber Mills for revenge."

"And to see Jenny."

He drew away far enough to look into her face. "And to see Jenny, find out if something was there. I won't lie. But I found you. And I fell for you, honey—just fell so fast and so hard, well there aren't words."

"For me? But I'm the town—"

"I know who you are. I know exactly who you are. Courageous and strong—strong enough to endure the unendurable. With a heart that can love despite all the blows. A woman who can hold her head up in a storm. One it's an honor for me to know."

Her eyes pooled with tears.

"Sarah, I know I don't deserve you. I've done things that should shame me. I came from near nothing, and I don't have much to offer you and your boy. But I reckon we've both been looking all our lives for a home. And if you'll be my home, darling, I'll swear most devoutly to be yours. Life long, if you'll have me."

"Well, Sean Hussey! That's quite a speech."

"I've been waiting days to offer you my heart. If you'll have it."

"Sean, I've loved you forever. Since we stood together on that station platform, I think. But I want you to be sure. If we stay here, life won't be easy. People are going to sneer at me. At you. Are you certain that's what you want?"

"I want you, honey. Wherever we are. If you and Luke are happy, the rest doesn't matter to me."

"Well, then. Well then!"

"I know you love this house."

"I surely do."

"And it's time—past time—you had something of

your own. I still hope Milo will come to his senses and take the farm. If not, I'll run it myself—from here if I need to."

"You'd do that for me?"

"I'd do anything for you."

Slowly, not even feeling the discomfort, he sank to one knee, clutching her hands. "Sarah Rupert, will you marry me?"

A hint of mischief gleamed in her eyes. "Become Sarah Hussey?"

"Please." Please God.

"Mrs. Hussey." She mused over it. "Whatever will this town make of that?"

With a laugh of joy he got to his feet and kissed her. For better or worse, they'd find out. Together. Because after his long journey, at last he'd come home.

A word about the author…

Laura Strickland enjoys researching interesting new settings for her books. Married, with one grown daughter, she has also mothered several rescue dogs and is intensely interested in animal welfare. Her love of dogs and her lifelong interest in Celtic history, magic and music, are all reflected in her writing.

Thank you for purchasing
this publication of The Wild Rose Press, Inc.

For questions or more information
contact us at
info@thewildrosepress.com.

The Wild Rose Press, Inc.